T0128859

JIGGLES, ROLF, AND THE REMARKABLE FINALE TO FRANK STONE'S CAREER

Wendell A. Duffield

JIGGLES, ROLF, AND THE REMARKABLE FINALE TO FRANK STONE'S CAREER

This is a work of fiction. All of the characters, names, incidents, organizations, and dialogue in this novel are either the products of the author's imagination or are used fictitiously.

iUniverse books may be ordered through booksellers or by contacting:

iUniverse
1663 Liberty Drive
Bloomington, IN 47403
www.iuniverse.com
1-800-Authors (1-800-288-4677)

Because of the dynamic nature of the Internet, any web addresses or links contained in this book may have changed since publication and may no longer be valid. The views expressed in this work are solely those of the author and do not necessarily reflect the views of the publisher, and the publisher hereby disclaims any responsibility for them.

Any people depicted in stock imagery provided by Thinkstock are models, and such images are being used for illustrative purposes only. Certain stock imagery © Thinkstock.

ISBN: 978-1-4917-6917-1 (sc)
ISBN: 978-1-4917-6918-8 (e)

Print information available on the last page.

iUniverse rev. date: 06/05/2015

PREFACE

My inspiration for writing this tale stems from the fact that the Colorado River in Grand Canyon National Park was repeatedly dammed when lava flows of nearby volcanoes spilled into and partly filled that remarkably deep trench. This action occurred between 800,000 and 100,000 years ago — equivalent to a human "mere moments ago" when compared to the age of planet Earth. As a geologist who has spent decades studying volcanoes, I see no reason to think that this hot canyon history has come to an end. Once set in motion, volcanically active areas typically persist for millions of years.

John Wesley Powell was the first trained scientist to study remnants of the lava dams, during his 1869 boat trip through the Grand Canyon. Since then, extending to current research projects, many other geologists have added to Powell's observations. I thank them all for providing the background grist that I have projected forward to create a fictional, though plausible, tale.

I also thank Karen Holmberg, Todd Berger, Richard McCallum, and Louella Holter for their many helpful editorial comments on a succession of drafts of the manuscript as it morphed into its final shape. My patient wife Anne has allowed me to spend boodles of my ongoing "retirement" hours at a computer keyboard, rather than enjoying more time with her in shared recreation.

I alone am responsible for inaccuracies and nonsense that readers of this tale may identify.

Cover photo: Oblique aerial view across the Grand Canyon, looking northeast. The dark hill in the center of the photo is Vulcan's Throne, a basalt cinder-cone volcano. The dark surface below and to the left are basalt lava flows that veneer tan-to-pinkish horizontal layers of ancient sedimentary rocks of the canyon walls.

OTHER BOOKS BY WENDELL A. DUFFIELD

Nonfiction:

Volcanoes of Northern Arizona: Sleeping Giants of the Grand Canyon Region

Chasing Lava: A Geologist's Adventures at the Hawaiian Volcano Observatory

From Piglets to Prep School: Crossing a Chasm

Poems, Song Lyrics, Essays, and Short Stories by Nina Hatchitt Duffield: Edited and annotated by Wendell and Anne Duffield

What's So Hot About Volcanoes?

Fiction:

When Pele Stirs: A Volcanic Tale of Hawaii, Hemp, and High-Jinks

Yucca Mountain Dirty Bomb

1

ENNUI

Early May

RING! RINNG!! RINNNG!!! A 2:00-PM-announcing shrill bell sounded across campus, echoing inside and outside the buildings. In seemingly synchronized timing, Franklin Stone, geology PhD, pushed back from his desk, leaned into his chair, and swiveled away from his PC monitor for a better view out the ground-level window of his office. The swivel elicited the squeak of metal on metal. Stone's chair was WWII vintage, and had become U.S. Government surplus after that war — gray iron frame, four roller-capped legs, frayed padding on armrests and backrest, and a tan seat cushion split down the center from long overuse. Doctor Stone might think that Ike once sat in this chair while developing invasion plans for D-day, though bothering to ship such a common piece of office furniture back to the USA from post-WWII Europe seemed a bit of a stretch. But the typically fun-loving Frank Stone realized that the chair likely had been the roost for a nondescript stateside clerk.

Most of Stone's office furnishings were government surplus. The Department of Defense regularly offered excess property to other federal agencies, including the U.S. Geological Survey, where Stone had worked for nearly thirty-five years before moving across town to Northern Arizona University in Flagstaff. If people like Stone didn't take this stuff, it would usually be trashed. Stone's agency in the federal government family had never seen the kind of lavish funding that regularly went to Defense. Hand-me-downs were a part of a USGS job. And after so many years

1

together, the chair and Stone were bonded buddies, wherever he happened to work.

His position at NAU was Adjunct Professor, an unpaid, honorary academic seat. With the title came an office, library privileges, and access to free flu shots when the annual ague and drippy-nose season rolled around. His duties included an occasional guest lecture in a full professor's classroom, serving as a member of advisory committees for graduate students, leading one-day field trips to local geological wonders, and being an experienced resource for students to discuss both academic and personal issues.

Stone often jokingly described his adjunct professor status as best summarized by the sound of the second syllable of the adjective. In fact, most of Stone's time was consumed by field-related research projects that the USGS didn't consider worth funding. Too academic, was the turndown reason then. Now, he was super pleased to have a university platform to pursue the research of his choosing.

He teetered and almost toppled for lack of a fifth roller-capped leg, a safety feature required on modern office chairs. He reached out and grasped the window ledge for support. To ease the discomfort for his weakened-with-age buttocks pressed against his pelvic bones, Stone kept the frayed original seat cushion covered with a square piece cut from a thick fluffy blanket. Still uncomfortable and a bit hazardous though it was, this chair was the intellectual hothouse from which numerous plans had been germinated for new forays into yet uncharted fields of geology throughout his professional career.

A sidewalk paralleled the building just a few feet outside Stone's office. Window open, he could almost touch pedestrians, and had often been tempted to do so when certain recognizable coeds paraded by. Within seconds, the whole gamut of students in a colorfully wide display of sizes, shapes, and clothing would add to his scenery on their hasty trips between classrooms for still more final exams. The scent and feel of spring was in the forested mountain air and summertime freedom from the academic grind filled their daydreams, suppressing thoughts about math equations, chemical formulas, Spanish vocabulary, and the multiple meanings subtly hidden in the words of famous authors. A few students might even be mentally reviewing facts about Stone's career-long subject — volcanoes.

He picked at a swollen, penny-sized white spot that had recently appeared on the back of his right hand. A layer of skin came off, exposing something almost pinkish — and maybe healthy. A patch of new hide for his mature Caucasian covering? He was aware that a career of working outside under the sun was a proven way to hatch skin cancer. And he'd been out there in blazing solar radiation for decades, chasing volcanoes on every one of Earth's continents, plus a bevy of oceanic islands, ranging from Arctic to tropical settings.

He had turned sixty-five just a week earlier. Compared to most males his age, he was still pretty well physically preserved, though not spared features of the deterioration process. *Even the most resistant volcanic lavas weather and turn to loose grit with time and exposure to the elements*, he reflected.

By age twenty Stone had already grown to stand a bit above six feet tall. He'd remained that lofty for decades. Then starting at about sixty, when his age went up, height went down. Negative correlation. The once six-foot-two college basketball player was now five feet eleven, or thereabouts. His weight tracked the age trend, in steadily rising positive correlation, but he wasn't yet heavy enough that he had to buy clothes for the stout man. He'd measure his height and weight later today, when he got home, and plot the new data on his life graph.

Stone was that kind of scientist — always measuring and charting things and looking for correlations. Then came the difficult part of interpreting his gaggle of graphs. A key to advancing his science was determining if there was a cause-and-effect link between co-changing variables. Or was an obvious mathematical correlation simply another potentially misleading fact, like noting that all criminals drank milk as children. Only an idiot would prohibit milk for children based on that link. Thinking about such stuff helped Stone feel alert and maybe even useful to society.

Student-watching helped him feel better preserved and younger than his true numerical age and flaky skin might suggest. It also rekindled fond memories of his days as an undergrad student at college back in the Upper Midwest. He briefly closed his eyes to invite visions of autumn weekend coed parties in the arboretum adjacent to campus. He chuckled, pulled a red handkerchief from a hip pocket, dabbed it with his tongue, and began rubbing the window glass. "Gotta get the maintenance crew to wash my office windows more often," he mumbled. Stone was thoroughly heterosexual — and a functional sexagenarian. The perfect ten he had focused on and successfully courted in college was still his satisfied, and equally amorous, wife.

But something seemed missing from his current life. Stone had drifted into bouts of depression that appeared to correlate with a slower pace of living and the wear and tear of so many years. These bouts struck and disappeared, never lasting more than a few hours at a time. Yet they kept recurring even though he strived to will them to cease. He hadn't yet overtly shared these troubling and confusing times with anyone, not even Bonnie, his wife of forty-five years. He was pretty sure, though, that she could see through his pseudo-macho veneer.

While Stone studied rocks as an undergrad, Bonnie had majored in the soft science called sociology. It seems she had effectively soaked up every bit of human-behavior wisdom that field had to offer. Within a few months after their marriage, Stone realized that Bonnie needed very few conversational encounters, even with strangers, for her well-informed evaluating mind to accurately analyze a personality and its foibles. Stone supposed that she had made some bad calls along the way, but he had never been able to fool her about what was on his mind, at any time in any situation. That had helped keep their relationship honest, and accounted for a marriage that had lasted longer than those for many of their college schoolmates.

Nicely meshed careers was another factor in a successful marriage. Stone traveled all around the world for his volcano projects, and finished each with a technical peer-reviewed paper published in a science journal. Bonnie wrote well-illustrated travel stories for a general readership, drawn from information gathered while traveling with her husband. She had syndicated columns in two national newspapers, and she contributed to several travel-related magazines. *Bouncing with Bonnie* was a widely known catchphrase in popular travel literature. And bouncing was a rough-ride feature of each of her stories. Stone traveled in anything but smooth-moving conveyances during his projects — camels, mules, single-engine aircraft, rapids-running rafts, horses, helicopters, snowmobiles, ATVs, 4x4

Jeeps, and such. The attendant bouncing had produced a few bruises to Bonnie's bottom along the way.

Bonnie had incredible talent for writing captivating tales in the normally dreaded (by stodgy traditional editors) second-person voice. This way, her readers were always the protagonists — the persons described by action verbs adorned with colorful adjectives, adverbs, and prepositional phrases. Her fans loved this style of adventure. Her editors also came to love her second-person tales, once they saw their sales rise with each issue containing a *Bouncing with Bonnie* piece.

Of course, behind each of her essays were the personal details of travel and adventure that she and Stone shared. But that information was for her diary — never for public consumption. Bonnie fiercely protected all the details of her private life. She shared her diary with Frank when he asked, but with no one else.

Given that he and Bonnie were together constantly while making their living from the products of joint travels and writing, Stone was sure that she was aware of his current occasional fits of malaise. Typically, though, she'd let him try to work out any downer on his own. Face-to-face verbal coaching, if she decided it was necessary, would come later.

Looking beyond wanderings of the mind, including childish fantasies of what was within reach just outside the window, Stone's physical body was on a somewhat steeper downward trend than his mind. Yes, there were the skin worries and the downs and ups in height and weight. Those were superficial in more than one sense. But although the simple act of walking was still easy enough, no one should expect him to run more than a couple of paces on his titanium-steel left knee. As he rubbed his hand across that surgery's scar hidden beneath denim jeans, he could feel the hard welt across his kneecap. He feared it would soon have a right knee companion. Decades of mornings spent scrambling up steep mountain slopes followed by afternoon descents with a rock-filled backpack had pretty much destroyed the soft tissue of his knee joints.

With three years of x-ray images in hand, *"It's finally bone-on-bone,"* his doctor had said the day she recommended surgery. A straight-talking unforgettable dynamo of an MD, Doctor Sally Crandall stood four-foot-ten in high heels, if she ever wore such shoes. She needed a stool to reach operating-table height. Small in physical stature, yes, but a talented and outspoken physician. When during his post-op physical therapy it became apparent that Stone's left leg was now just a bit shorter than before, Doctor Crandall joked, "Your politics have always been obvious. Now you're just a bit more left leaning." Stone and Crandall shared a laugh over that truism. She was as refreshingly blunt and honest as Bonnie.

Bouts with gout came and went with his irregular consumption of booze, a positive correlation whose data he refused to formally graph. Confirming cause and effect could be scary and unwanted! Inward-facing crooks in the outer joints of now arthritic index and little fingers were bothersome, but not overly painful. He was especially grateful that his spine was pain free and erect, after so many field seasons of carrying heavy backpacks.

Gettin' old sucks, he mused while rocking in his noisy chair, temporarily shedding years by eyeing the student parade. He stopped the source of the squeak. *No sense actin' out the rockin' chair part of old age till that's the only way I can get exercise.* Realistically, Stone's physical condition was typical of most old field geologists who hadn't been slackers. He just didn't want to admit and accept that truism.

Within a few minutes, student traffic thinned to a normal midterm level. Stone swiveled back to face his government surplus desk, which was tucked into a corner of his square space. The office was much the worse for wear than its occupant. The room measured twelve by twelve feet — the standard size for NAU geology professors. The sheetrock covering the walls was pitted, disfigured, and discolored by nails, tacks, and tape used by a series of occupants who had hung maps and such there. Tan eight-inch-square, heavily worn linoleum tiles, each decorated with a geometric design, veneered the floor. The installer had failed to recognize that an overall pattern was meant to flow from tile to tile. Most tiles were badly scuffed, with curled broken edges probably from decades of moving office furniture in and out and from one wall to another.

He focused on the desktop where a few printed pages of an unfinished manuscript about a small volcano just east of Flagstaff stared up at him, practically shouting *Work on me!* When completed and in print, this would wrap up his current project. An ominous question that haunted his mind was, *Would it be the last?* He hoped not, but unlike during the earlier years of his career, he now had no new entries on a to-do research list he kept tacked to the wall behind his desk. For the first time, ever, all entries were crossed off. This bugged him. He badly wanted at least one more idea there waiting to be addressed with vigor and enthusiasm once he was finished with the current study. He longed for another field and intellectual challenge before his professional bucket list was empty, before admitting it was time to retire into the sedentary existence that sixty plus years of age would invite.

He arranged the manuscript pages into a neat stack. He'd tackle that project tomorrow. It was about a lava flow that had spilled into and dammed up the canyon of the Little Colorado River just east of Flagstaff. A noteworthy outcome was creation of a tourist-attracting waterfall the height of Niagara. Neat stuff. Stone's research showed that the eruption was so young that ancestors of today's Navajo and Hopi people may have watched the show. His geology colleagues, archaeologists, anthropologists and other readers would probably enjoy the tale. But once he'd finished the writing and it was formally in print, what then?

He stared at the wall, focusing on nothing, feeling a bit morose, too morose, chewing on a torn fingernail, wishing to once again be the younger geologist who could scale the tallest volcano to probe and understand its secrets. He sighed, reached forward, and pushed the OFF button of his PC.

He decided to go home now, early, mix himself a rum and Coke, plus a gin and tonic for Bonnie — her favorite high-octane drink. Maybe that would loosen her up to the state that she'd share her analysis of what was causing his troubled moods. Stone's mind veered off on a tangent.

I wish I was as strong as her, both mentally and physically. She's only two years younger than me, but her mind and body have changed little from what captivated me during our college years. Five foot two. Eyes of blue that sparkle and shine. She carries no excess poundage, has a head topped by a nest of strikingly tousled naturally black hair, and can out-walk me on our summer Sunday afternoon hikes in the forest behind our house. Maybe it's her yoga and yogurt.

Stone stood, ran fingers through his thinning stringy gray hair, exhaled a grunt-like noise, pinched the bicycle-tire ridge of soft flesh that encircled his waist, just above the belt, and prepared to walk home.

2

AN ODD COUPLE

A few seconds later:

As Stone was stuffing his empty lunch bucket and a few to-be-read papers into a small tan weathered backpack, someone rapped on the office door. "Come in," he yelled as he zipped up the pack.

He turned and watched Richard Stewart, a University of Utah PhD and the department's earthquake professor, push open the door and step quietly in, wearing his trademark Nikes. *I wonder what's up,* Stone thought. *Stewart rarely comes calling on me. We mix about as well as oil and water.*

Stewart was toting a long four-inch-diameter cylindrical cardboard tube, the kind used to carry rolled-up maps and sometimes used by geology students as dueling weapons in playful mock space-alien battles. He closed the door firmly behind him, apparently wanting privacy.

Like Stone, he was dressed in professor casual, although his attire didn't have the three-day look typical of Stone's duds. Only department chairpersons dressed formally, in keeping with a code practiced by all upper-level university administrative employees. For the current geology chairperson, that meant a dress or a conservative skirt topped with a tasteful blouse. Dress-down Fridays allowed her to wear something in the jumpsuit category. Teaching-and-research geologists weren't known for sartorial splendor any day of the week.

Stewart was in his early fifties, of fair complexion, six-foot four, and topped with short sandy hair, plus reading glasses perched on a narrow-bridge nose. Long legs carried the trim physique of a devoted jogger.

Weather permitting, he ran four miles along forest trails early each morning, before his teaching duties.

The department joke was that Stewart always jogged past one of his seismometers, closely enough that his footfalls would record as earthquakes. Northern Arizona had a few non-human-caused earth shakes from time to time. But those times were commonly separated by years. Arizona was no California with its San Andreas and myriad other faults, at least one of which twitched enough to shake a seismometer or two or more every day.

Unlike Stone and other rock-pounding field geologists, the research of the NAU seismologist depended on earth becoming restless to the point of natural shaking and sometimes breaking. Once his seismometers were deployed here and there across northern Arizona and rigged to automatically broadcast their findings back to his office, Stewart could only sit in his chair and wait for earth to convulse on its own. No quake meant nothing to work with — at least of local origin.

So he spent most of his time analyzing the records of quakes originating elsewhere on Earth, shakes that were strong enough to travel from the far side of the planet and record in Flagstaff. These biggies gave him enough information to use in classroom exercises.

Still, the Geology Department was threatened with losing their seismologist faculty position, as a state-mandated budgetary move. The thinking of legislators in Phoenix was that earth science spending could and should be shaved by focusing seismic research and teaching at only one of the three state universities. Historically, when this kind of push came to shove, NAU being the smallest of the three had the least leverage to torque the system to its advantage. Stone knew that Stewart and the Department Chair were in the midst of working feverishly to convince the elected money managers that the northern part of their state was where earthquakes were most likely to occur and so seismic studies should be focused at NAU, the campus nearest the anticipated action.

"Got a minute, Franklin?" Stewart blurted. He seemed agitated, excited, a bit short of breath — not his normally calm, deferential, and some might even say boring self. Stone was about to learn why.

"Yeah. Sure, Dick," Stone said. "I was just gettin' ready to head home a bit early. But I can stay awhile. No problem."

He dropped his pack and pointed to the office's only other chair. Another surplus rescue.

"Have a seat," Stone said.

Stewart preferred to stand, clutching the cardboard tube, shifting his weight from foot to foot.

"So, what's up? You're actin' like the earthquake guy who just successfully rode out a magnitude-eight shake and lived to talk about it. Most of us other folks would be scared spitless by that kind of action. But you quake guys live for the big one."

Stone covered his mouth with an open hand to hide the orifice for a loud yawn.

Stewart began to explain his behavior.

"If I'm a bit twitchy it's because of a tiny shake, not a building breaker. Actually I'm excited by what seems to be lots of tiny shakes, maybe hundreds, thousands."

Stewart was having an increasingly difficult time standing still. It reminded Stone of a sort of unease that he'd read about in a recent issue of *Seniors Magazine* that had mysteriously appeared in his department mailbox — something that visited old men with frequent unexpected urges to urinate. He hoped to never be so afflicted. And Stewart was too young for that kind of malady.

"What are you talkin' about?" said Stone. "I follow the geology news for our part of the world. There hasn't been a word for months about earthquakes."

Stewart was cradling the tube like he might his two-month-old son. He was Mormon and the new family member was number seven — five boys and two girls. He had that many reasons, and perhaps a few more in the hopper, to very much want to keep his teaching position. He had the security of tenure, but that didn't mean spit if the position itself was axed.

Stewart smiled. "Well, I think you'll be very interested in what I've got to show you," he said. "I'll have to roll out some maps to explain what I'm talking about. I'm hoping your early career experiences at Kilauea will help me determine if my interpretation of what's happening with one of my seismometers is crazy — or a sign of possibly big things to come."

Stewart sensed that by mentioning Kilauea he now had Stone's attention. He paused to allow a broad enigmatic smile grow across his face. "There could be a research gold mine here," he said while brandishing the map tube. "For both of us."

He then glanced upward, in what Stone knew was not meant for a better view of the cobweb-draped fluorescent light fixtures, and added, "There may be a job-saving gift from above for me. And something that can add another fancy feather or two in *your* professional bonnet."

Stewart was now almost whispering, like he thought the NSA might be listening in.

"I haven't yet talked with anyone else about this stuff," he said. "No one."

Mention of his decades-earlier career experiences with an active volcano in Hawaii had indeed piqued Stone's curiosity. But what hot news could this master of the cool calm and collected possibly have to share that would relate to those years? And why the jittery secretiveness?

Stewart had the reputation of never showing emotions beyond uncanny, some would say bland, steadiness. He was an imperturbable Mormon family man. He could have played the role of the Latter Day Saint proselytizer who had visited Stone's house last weekend — that young, pasty-skinned, trim man, dressed in dark, well-pressed slacks, a white shirt, and a monochromatic Windsor-knot tie. That young man with short, neatly combed hair walked quietly away when Stone interrupted the pitch to join his flavor of the supernatural by shouting, "All organized religions are BS! Enemies of science!" Mr. Mormon had simply voiced a polite, "Thank you for your time, sir. Have a nice day," and then turned away and headed toward the next house on the street.

Yes, the Stewart that Stone knew could and probably would do that, too. But now he seemed almost out of control enough to wet himself.

"Okay, Dick," Stone said. "Let's lay out your baby so you can show me what's got your undies in a knot."

When Stewart frowned at that comment, Stone knew that he'd hit the hot button he'd aimed for.

Stone stood, opened the door, and waited for Stewart to follow. They walked across a hall that separated the one-story building into two long rows of rooms, to a communal office where the only piece of furniture was a large table, positioned in the middle of the twelve-by-twelve space.

Cardboard boxes overflowing with rock samples, fieldwork gear and such occupied much of the surrounding space in obstacle-course disarray.

Stewart closed the door and locked it behind them. He extracted two maps from the tube. He separated the two and leaned one into a corner. He placed the other on the table. They held it flat and weighted down the corners with buckshot-filled tan leather pouches that were on the table for just such a purpose.

The flattened sheet was an ordinary contour map, a staple variety that last-generation field geologists, like Stone, used to quickly see the physical lay of the land. It covered much of the northern third of Arizona. Closely spaced parallel lines of elevation clearly defined the deep trench of the Colorado River. Like the river, they appeared to flow down from the northeast and then curve to a westerly trend across the core of Grand Canyon National Park. The surrounding landscape was pretty flat, very flat by comparison with a five-thousand–foot–deep canyon.

"Give me a hand please," Stewart said, pointing to the knob of a setscrew at Stone's corner of the table. Each worked his side and locked the table surface at enough of an incline for easier map viewing.

The map featured eight red dots, more-or-less equally spaced over the landscape. Stewart pulled a pencil-shaped laser pointer from a shirt pocket, played its beam here and there on the map, and said, "These dots are the locations of the seismometers that transmit their recordings back to my office. I've always wanted a few more instruments for more complete coverage, but the budget? You know that situation."

Stone watched and listened quietly, hoping for some sort of punchline that would explain Stewart's mood and need for secrecy. So far the show-and-tell was as dry and unsurprising as finding the parched bones of a coyote cow kill on some arid landscape.

"I may not have showed you this map before," Stewart continued. "I want you to see that my seismic network covers a big swath of terrain. Any quakes of significant magnitude in the region should register on several of the instruments. Something like a magnitude-three shake, or more powerful."

"Agreed," Stone said, in a dry matter-of-fact tone. "I've seen a map like this — maybe even this one — posted on the hallway wall outside your office door." So far the show-and-tell was boring.

"Okay, so here's the thing. Please listen," Stewart said in a near whisper. "I've got evidence of quakes, lots of quakes that are shaking at only one place, affecting only one of the jugs."

Stone recognized the term "jug" in Stewart's context as slang for a seismometer. Apparently, early versions of these earthquake-sensing devices had been about the size and shape of a water jug. And jug was a lot easier to say than seismometer. So modern digital electronic versions, though different in appearance, went by the same term. *Such common words from the lips of Stewart,* he mused. *He must be buzzed.*

Stewart stared at Stone and continued, speaking with hiss-like intensity. "It's happened many times during the past several months. Each burst lasts for something like minutes on up to an hour." His right hand became as animated as his low voice, as an index finger wagged up and down as it tracked along an imagined horizontal line. "At first I thought maybe a big rig truck or two or more were rumbling by for some construction project. But there aren't any roads close enough to this jug for that to happen."

Stone's nod told Stewart that he now had his colleague's attention.

"Then I figured maybe extra strong winds were the source of the shaking. But if so, more than one instrument should have registered the blow. That didn't happen. Besides, when I checked the records of weather conditions, the shaking didn't correlate with times of unusually strong wind velocity."

Stewart's voice was still a whisper. But his words were coming faster.

"Hey! Slow down or you'll give yourself a heart fart," Stone said. Despite this snarky comment, Stewart's mention of the possibility of some cause and effect correlation, in this case a lack thereof, genuinely piqued Stone's attention.

"Okay. So which of those jugs has been jigglin'?" Stone asked.

Stewart stopped the finger wag and pointed the laser beam to a red dot within a relatively isolated part of Grand Canyon National Park — a place called Toroweap. "Here," he said, and then went silent, waiting for a reaction from Stone. And there was indeed a huge *aha!* reaction in Stone. But he chose to keep it internalized for now, voicing only a noncommittal *hmmmm* as he scratched his chin.

Stone knew this patch of ground well. He'd spent many days there during the past few years. It was home to hundreds of basalt volcanoes, geologically young volcanoes, that decorated the North Rim of the canyon and a few miles beyond across an area called the Uinkaret Plateau. Geologically young to Stone meant Quaternary, a term geologists use to encompass the most recent two million years of Earth's multi-billion-year history. One of those Quaternary basalt cinder cones was so young that Native Americans had watched the eruption. In wonder? In fear? Blobs of the erupting molten basalt had plopped down on their pottery. So maybe fear was indeed in the air when that happened. It was pretty easy and quite logical to imagine people dropping their water and food pots as they fled a fountain of fire-like molten rock splashing on the ground around them.

Stewart knew about that eruption. And now Stone understood why Stewart wanted to share his discovery with him, whatever the explanation for seismometer shaking might turn out to be. Stone was the only department geologist experienced in studying active volcanoes. The entire Big Island of Hawaii is made of basalt, and that's where Stone had figuratively cut his volcano teeth, to say nothing about the real cuts of his flesh — there on Kilauea's broken-up glassy lavas. He had watched more than one eruption unfold. Stewart wanted to be educated on all the geologic trimmings that go with that kind of experience.

Silence. Then Stone checked his wristwatch.

"Look. I promised Bonnie I'd get home early today," he lied. "Let's huddle again tomorrow, in the morning. In my office."

Stone pointed to the corner. "Bring that other map, too, or whatever it is. And bring copies of seismograms, the charts that show the traces of the shakin' you're so excited about. I've got an idea or two of what might be jigglin' that jug of yours, but I want to sleep on it for a night. If I'm right, it has nothin' to do with the weather or a huge semi or two truckin' nearby, or anything else at the surface. I'm thinkin' of somethin' hidden."

Stewart's facial expression registered excitement — quickly followed by disappointment. He'd have to wait until tomorrow to hear what Stone was thinking now. Mormon patience kicked in.

"Okay. Tomorrow then." He rolled up the two maps, and carefully inserted them into the carrying tube. He and Stone releveled the tabletop, exited, and closed the door behind them. Stewart headed down the hall to his office. Stone retrieved his backpack, locked his office and began what would be an exciting mile-long-walk home. He had explosive project possibilities to mull over along the way. His artificial knee wouldn't mind this stroll.

With each stride, Stone imagined a new entry for his bucket list. And that was so very important to him. He'd begun and organized his career, a wet-behind-the-ears new PhD, by posting a handwritten list of to-do projects on the wall behind his office desk. He crossed off projects as he finished them. New ones were then added. He also kept a copy of the list in a galvanized steel bucket purchased with his first professional salary check. It was a classic upward-flaring round thing, topped with a hinged handle. He now kept that symbolic bucket at his home office, because the damn NAU janitors insisted on emptying it on their daily rounds. At the moment, the list had only the Little Colorado River project. And that would soon be crossed off.

But now, with the news from Stewart, he conjured up a slow but strong winding down of his volcanic career, a going out with a bang heard all around Arizona, maybe even around the nation if not the world. He was anxious to share this news with Bonnie, who would greet him at the door when he got home. She would find him more like the young Frank Stone — her college beau — when he charged through the door, grabbed her in a tight hug, and planted a tongue-twisting wet kiss on her partly open lips before he explained his reason for such enthusiasm.

3

A PLAN TAKES SHAPE

Eight AM the next day:

Stewart, dressed in fresh conservative clothes, clean shaven, looking alert and with map tube in hand, paced impatiently at Stone's office door. A half hour later Stone arrived, in yesterday's attire now even more deeply wrinkled, face covered with a twenty-four-hour gray stubble. He yawned, scratched an armpit, and said, "Didn't get enough sleep last night. Too much excitement, I guess." That excitement was only partly what Stewart imagined it to be.

He keyed his office door, entered, and got a pot of coffee perking. Stewart was sipping some variety of pale yellow tea — presumably herbal — from a clear glass cup.

"Let's use the common room again," Stone said. "I assume we'll want the table."

They crossed the hall and reset the tabletop to yesterday's better-map-viewing tilt. "Lay out that second map you had yesterday so I can see what's there," Stone said.

While Stewart spread out the map, pinning it down with the shot-filled leather pouches, Stone went back to his office and poured hot, very black caffeinated coffee into a colorful ceramic mug emblazoned with "Volcanoes Rule." It was a handcrafted gift from Mindy, one of his cutest graduate student advisees. He added a heaping teaspoon of sugar-in-the-raw and stirred to mellow the acrid coffee taste.

On the way back across the hall, he encountered Dave Jones, the department's geophysics professor, and Christina Mender, the NAU paleontologist. They both joked about how unusually early it was to see an adjunct professor at the office. "Got a date with Stewart," Stone said, pointing to the partly open common-room door. Then in a lower voice, "Wouldn't wanna stand him up, ya know."

Dave and Chris smiled, gave a thumbs up, and whispered, "Have a fun time with the party animal." They continued down the hall toward their twelve by twelve spaces.

Stewart closed the door as soon as Stone walked in. Seems he wanted to maintain the same level of yesterday's secrecy. He had laid out the second map. Hot drinks in hand, the show-and-tell began.

"This is an enlargement of the area where the one jug has been shaking," Stewart explained. "The geology is an overlay on the contoured base map."

"I don't need this kind of primer," Stone quipped. It was a conventional geologic map. It showed a four-mile-wide block of ground bounded on two sides by vertical north/south faults, those breaks in the earth that formed during episodes of ancient earthquake shaking. The south boundary was the Grand Canyon slot with the Colorado River at the bottom. At the north, the map ended where the cover of volcanoes and their lava flows petered out, atop ancient horizontal sedimentary layers.

Stone noisily sipped his hot Joe, spilling a couple drops on the map. He dried them with a crumpled red bandana from a hip pocket. "You've gotta know that I'm familiar with this," he said in exaggerated disbelief. Stone was half of a two-man team that had mapped the area several years earlier. He was coauthor of the published monograph of their efforts. He and his USGS colleague George B had done the work before Stone left the USGS for NAU.

"Yes. You're right," Stewart said. "I know that. Guess I'm too excited and wrapped up in this to remember the obvious." He hesitated before continuing his introduction.

"I've only been out there once," Stewart admitted, "to help install the seismometer. I hadn't really thought about the place since then — until the shaking began. The place is so remote. It's like starting from scratch for me. A technician drives up to take care of periodic maintenance of the jug."

Part of the map area, for a few miles northward from the river, was the Toroweap section of Grand Canyon National Park. The balance was a tiny slice of vast public land overseen by the Bureau of Land Management. Much of the land covered by Stewart's map was forested with patches of drought-resistant juniper, pinyon and ponderosa pine. The rest was simply high desert shrubbery.

Save for a national park ranger, permanent human population of the region was zero. The ranger lived in a small cabin. Non-electronic connections to the outside world were via an adjacent dirt landing strip that could accommodate small single-engine-land planes, or by a fifty-mile drive northward over a rarely-maintained dirt road to the nearest pavement. Once on that pavement, it was another ten miles east to the first town, Fredonia, Arizona. At Toroweap, radio and phone communications were possible via satellite links. A propane-powered generator provided electricity. Trucks hauled water in when rain catchment wasn't adequate.

Beef cows populated the BLM land — way too many, environmentalists insisted. The hoofed bovines overran the ground, munching up anything greenish that was chewable and digestible, while trampling almost every other living thing into dusty death.

"The jug of interest is near the youngest of the volcanoes that you and George mapped," Stewart continued. "That's the one that Native Americans watched when it erupted. I chose that spot because it's not far from a Jeep track. It's pretty easy to get equipment in there. Also, I thought maybe that young volcano ground could still be restless enough to give me some earthquake examples to use in the classroom."

"Makes sense to me," Stone said. "So now show me some of the seismograms from that jug — the squiggly tracings that have you so worked up."

Stewart shook several ten-by-twenty-inch paper sheets from the tube. There were six, stacked in time-sequence order — the oldest was at the bottom.

Maybe this earthquake guy knows some field geology after all, Stone mused. *He arranges his seismograms like layers of sedimentary rocks, the foundation under the frosting of lava at Toroweap.*

Stewart selected the bottom sheet. It was labeled May 10 of the previous year. They weighted down the corners.

The image had been printed from a digital file. Labels showed that it covered a twenty-four-hour period. Had there been no shaking of the jug, the record would be twenty-four horizontal lines, stacked vertically, with each representing one hour of recording. However, lines for 4:00 to 5:00 AM and 10:00 to 11 PM were a constant waveform. An almost identical tracing shape ran from the second half of 10:00 to 11:00 AM, then continuing until noon.

"Interesting," Stone said in a business-like voice, not tinged with his frequent use of sarcasm, peevishness, or playfulness. He tugged at his left earlobe, a sign of serious thought, recognizable by those who knew him well. "Very interesting. Show me more examples."

Coffee and tea finished, they set their cups aside. For the next hour, they studied the six seismograms. Each contained a few bursts of wavy tracing. Stone jotted down notes as they worked through the record pile. The most recent showed shaking just a month before Stone's recent birthday.

"I have many more examples back in my office, if you want to see them," Stewart said. "I just picked out a few over the time since this kind of recording began to appear."

Silence ensued as Stone pondered the data. His thoughts were awhirl with exciting possibilities. Stewart waited for his volcano expert to speak. Finally.

"A couple of questions," Stone said.

"Please ask," Stewart blurted.

"Any instrumental problems with electronics, with recording and sending the data to your office receivers, et cetera?" Stone began.

"No," Stewart quickly replied. Then in rapid-fire follow-on, their conversation continued.

"Any modifications to the field instrument, the jug, during the recording period?"

"No."

"So, these are records from an untweaked stable system."

"Yes."

Stoned stared at the room ceiling and started thinking out loud, projecting enough volume for Stewart to hear. "You've already eliminated weather and vehicular traffic as possible ground shakers. And no herd of stampeding cattle would record in this way."

He paused, thinking quietly. Then continued.

"The amplitude of the waves, top to bottom, is virtually constant," he said. "The periodicity of the wave traces stays in the range of roughly one to two cycles per second. I guess that's called one to two hertz in your lingo. And the wave patterns last for anywhere from seconds to minutes to hours." Another earlobe tug.

"So the ground is shakin' alright," Stone continued. "But not the way it does with conventional quakes. Those hit big, give huge up-and-down swings early on, and then quickly taper off and fade away. And they carry much much larger hertz numbers."

He rubbed his facial stubble, then said, "I've got an idea or two about what's goin' on. If I'm right, we're both gonna be pumped. But I don't wanna go on record yet, not even with secretive you."

Stone then began scratching his scalp with both hands, a behavior he often used to try to stimulate useful thoughts that might be trapped in his brain. Stewart stared at him, impatient for some significant bottom line, or at least some indication of what the volcano guy thought was happening.

Stone quickly focused a stare on Stewart. "Here's what we're gonna do next," he said, suddenly. "It's Friday. The semester is officially over at the end of today. Go to the department office right now and ask the secretary to reserve us a university motor-pool four-wheel-drive truck for next week. We're goin' to Toroweap Monday morning, first thing. A three-day trip will be long enough to scope things out. I hope your family can spare you for that long."

Stewart stood rigid, smiling, like an obedient motivated student getting marching orders from the professor.

"Bring sleeping gear," Stone continued. "We'll have to camp out for two nights. I'll get food. And I've got the equipment we'll need for cookin', carryin' drinking water and such. I'll bring a tent, even though it almost never rains up there this time of year. I'll google Mormon diet no-nos, and you should bring any special food and drink you want."

They shut down the common room. Stewart disappeared down the hallway toward his office, his gait an expression of elation.

Stone got on the website for the USGS Hawaiian Volcano Observatory and spent the rest of the day reviewing seismic records for times leading up to several past eruptions at Kilauea. *Maybe I'll bring some examples to show Stewart next week at Toroweap.* He closed his eyes, tensed his stomach muscles and felt a tremor of excitement stirring within his aging but still motivated body.

4

DISCOVERY FIELD TRIP

Seven AM Monday:

During a couple of phone conversations over the weekend, Stone and Stewart ironed out the details of their trip to Toroweap. Stone and Bonnie waited in the driveway for Stewart's arrival. He soon pulled in, driving a white 4x4 Ford Ranger emblazoned with *Northern Arizona University: Official Use Only.* Stone and Stewart loaded equipment into the spacious back compartment. Then Stone and Bonnie shared a farewell hug and kiss. Bonnie waved her goodbye from the front door stoop, as the geology duo headed out of Flagstaff on U.S. Highway 89, Stewart at the wheel.

Traffic moving north was light. Most drivers were commuting to jobs in Flagstaff from homes in a slipshod rural housing development called Doney Park — Donkey Park to detractors who decried the weak zoning ordinances, and the even weaker enforcement thereof. It seems that one person's neat and elegant castle out there was always adjacent to another man's junkyard.

Five miles out of Flag, a sign directed traffic eastward to visit Sunset Crater Volcano National Monument. This reminded Stone that he and Stewart were headed to the only other Arizona volcano young enough to have been indisputably viewed by Native Americans during eruption — the one named Little Springs for a water seep in what was basically desert country.

The Sunset Crater sign also reminded Stone that he had once publicly proposed a name change from Sunset to Sunrise Crater Volcano. During his visit to this area in 1887, John Wesley Powell suggested the Sunset name because reddish hues carried by cinders that mantle the top of the volcano's cone reminded him of a colorful sunset scene. And that suggestion stuck. However, Stone argued, in public lectures and with letters published in Flag's daily newspaper, that reddish hues are also prevalent in sunrise scenes, and that from his geological point of view, the volcano was a beginning, not an end — an introduction to what would be future historical nearby eruptions. And it lies to the east where the sun rises.

He had backed off this crusade when the Flagstaff Chamber of Commerce and other conservative business-minded traditionalists vociferously objected to his suggested name change. More than once, he had learned that reasoning with Flag's town fathers was likely to be about as productive as trying to convince Stewart that a literal translation of his Christian bible was so misleading to the real world we live in.

Stone chose not to start this kind of discussion now with Stewart. He'd tried before. Tried to understand how someone who believes the Earth is about six thousand years old can honestly pursue a profession whose cornerstone is a planet that's four and a half billion years old. *Too early in the day for a pertinent discussion of that sort.* They traveled in silence.

They continued north, dropping out of pine forest as they quickly lost a couple thousand feet of elevation. Some of the older six hundred cinder cones and their lava flows that are called the San Francisco Volcanic Field decorated the sagebrush landscape. Eventually, lava thinned and gave way to a thick horizontal stack of ancient sedimentary formations, eroded into small mesas and such — about where the highway entered the Navajo Indian Reservation. Nearly an hour out, they stopped at the Cameron Trading Post to stretch legs and change seats. It was a cloud-free, hot, and windy day — springtime in northern Arizona. They opened side windows partway for a bit of cooling breeze to counteract a blazing sun.

With Stone at the wheel, they crossed the bridge spanning the Little Colorado River. He peered down briefly and made a mental note that water flow looked to be minor compared to typical springtime runoff in the past. The relative drought that had come to the Southwest with global climate change was the cause.

Further north, over barren ground, then up and over the gentle Gap Pass, evidence of human presence was sparse. They passed a few makeshift roadside Navajo trinket shops there to lure in tourists, hogans with their doors facing eastward, and grazing shaggy Merino sheep tended by herd dogs and elderly women garbed in colorful skirts dragging in the dirt. Vistas to the right were shielded by the towering wall of the Echo Cliffs. Flatter ground stretched out as an irregular plateau to the west. Stewart read a book as Stone drove.

Stone steered onto Alt U.S. 89, where 89 swept into a curve that climbs steeply eastward on the way to Page, a town built during construction of the nearby Glen Canyon Dam.

They crossed Navajo Bridge, spanning the Colorado River five hundred feet below. They stopped at a visitor center to ease the urge so intricately described in the *Seniors Magazine* that someone had recently stuffed into Stone's NAU mailbox. Human radiators drained, they walked to the canyon rim and gazed down to the river. A tourist group in yellow rubber rafts floated by on their way into Grand Canyon National Park and its famous and challenging rapids. Drought or not, a certain amount of water was constantly released at Glen Canyon Dam — sustaining a liquid highway sufficient to feed those rapids.

Stone remained at the wheel as they climbed up and over the forested Kaibab Plateau that crested at the village of Jacob Lake, and then descended the west side of the plateau into Fredonia, their last chance for supplies. At a convenience store, they topped off the Ranger's fuel tank, while washing down snacks with cold drinks — Stone a Coke and Stewart a fruit juice. At the town center stoplight, where Alt U.S. 89 turned north, Stone drove straight through, westward on U.S. 389.

The silence was starting to grate on Stone. He liked to banter, be it on a serious topic or tongue-in-cheek fun. Leaving Fredonia, they were now in the heart of terrain called the Arizona Strip — the part of Arizona effectively isolated from the rest of the state by the Grand Canyon. This rural desolate geography was famous, or infamous depending on one's point of view, as a present-day bastion of multiple-wife Mormon fundamentalism. *Time to tweak Stewart*, he mused.

"Hey Dick," Stone said. "Do ya have family in Colorado City just up ahead a few miles?"

This town of a few hundred inhabitants was barely in Arizona, a stone's throw south of the state line with Utah. Stone and Bonnie had driven through many times on trips between Flagstaff and Cedar City, Utah, for weekends of entertaining theater performances. In its unique way, Colorado City architecture was impressive. A typical house there was a two-story large-footprint rectangle. Both levels were punctuated by regularly spaced windows, like a low-cost hotel or motel. The open secret, of course, was that a husband in Colorado City needed multiple bedrooms to accommodate his several wives and multitude of children.

"No. None," Stewart said quickly.

"Any friends there?" Stone persisted. "I understand it's one hundred percent Mormon."

"Nope, no friends. Don't know anyone there," Stewart insisted.

"I'll bet you heard about the latest raid by Arizona cops, hopin' to arrest bigamists. Was in all the state newspapers," Stone continued.

"Yes. Of course, I know about that," Stewart said in a voice tinged with exasperation. "I'm not interested in such gossipy stuff."

Off and on for years Arizona law enforcement had made attempts to arrest Colorado City bigamists. But an element of surprise usually was lacking, and all the wife-rich men had to do was walk a few yards into Utah, where they were welcome and safe from the law. Never mind that the current official Mormon Church position banned bigamy. Out of sight out of mind seemed to rule in such remote territory as the Arizona Strip and neighboring Utah.

"You Mormons sure do have an interesting religion," Stone said. "Latecomers to the Protestant flavor. Young, and like other religions, full of unbelievable tales. Unbelievable in the eyes of scientific testing anyway."

Stewart pretended to concentrate on his book. Stone wasn't ready to give up his prod.

"When and where was it that Joseph Smith discovered those founding stone tablets, or whatever they were, buried in upstate New York?" Stone asked.

Stewart refused to be drawn into another debate on religion with Stone. He'd been there before, and knew that Stone called himself a humanistic atheist who enjoyed opportunities to argue with those who believe in a supernatural being and the like. He fished out and opened a roadmap from the glove compartment in front of him. "You might want to slow down a bit. I think we're near the turn off to Toroweap," Stewart advised.

"I know," Stone said. "Been here before, ya know. Many a time."

Following a minute or two of silence, Stone turned left onto the rarely maintained one-lane dirt road that led to Toroweap. They were immediately enveloped in a dust cloud. He closed his window. Stewart followed suit. Stone turned on the air conditioner and they bounced forward in continuing silence.

Forty-six slow miles of bumps and dust later, they turned right onto a branch road, westward upslope to the base of Mount Trumbull, a tall mesa-like hill veneered with lava flows. Straight ahead southward another eight miles would have taken them into the national park. Little Springs Volcano was a couple miles south of Trumbull.

"We'll camp near your jigglin' jug tonight," Stone said. "I want to visit that instrument tomorrow to be sure it's the faithful recorder that you've described." Stone glanced right as Stewart closed his book, exposing the Book of Mormon cover inscription.

"Good," Stewart added. "I want that visit, too. Like I told you earlier, I've only been there once. The time my helper and I installed the jug."

"Check," Stone replied. "After that and a quick recon of the Little Springs lava flow, we'll visit the Toroweap Ranger Station. Maybe the backcountry ranger there felt some of your jug's jiggles."

The sun was near the horizon by the time they arrived at the western edge of the Little Springs lava flow. They had gained enough elevation to leave sagebrush for reentry into pine forest. Stone stopped at a flat patch of ground where sleeping would be comfortable. He gathered some wood for a campfire. Stewart busied himself setting up a small tent.

They ate simply, sitting next to the fire. Conversation was limited to *tastes fine, enough* and such. Fact is, they shared so few common interests, beyond geology. And even on that topic, there were opposing views of fundamental stuff. Like the age of the Earth and all the fascinating events that had transpired to the present.

Stewart retreated into the privacy of the tent as soon as he finished eating. Stone suspected that he didn't want certain undergarments to become a topic of discussion. Stone could see the glow of a headlamp through the walls of the tent. *He's probably reading from the Book of Mormon. He should have it memorized by now.*

Stewart had an extended family and his religion. Stone had Bonnie, no children, a diminishing number of living relatives, and distaste for organized religion. So what does one do when there's no TV to watch, no Internet for entertainment, and you didn't bring a book to read?

Stone sat near the dwindling fire, closed his eyes, and focused his thoughts on life with Bonnie. *What a trip it's been. We started on a path a bit like Stewart's. Not the religion part. The children part. Had plans for four kids, once I finished my PhD. But by then we were having way too much fun together, just the two of us with our careers, to want to get tied down with raisin' kids. Selfish? Don't know. But we also figured that planet Earth already had plenty of people — maybe even too many. Eventually, Bonnie got worried about possible long-term effects of takin' birth-control pills. So it was off to Doctor Lewis's operating room for me. Still have those two short sections of vas deferens, sealed in transparent plastic cubes. They stare at me every time I open the medicine cabinet at home. Still think we made the right decision, though, when I had those sperm tubes clipped.*

He stopped reminiscing, and looked skyward. The Big Dipper seemed perched atop Trumbull. It was upright, promising to spill no rain to those who believed in such nonsense. Stone laid out a tarp and sleeping bag on the ground. Somewhere nearby an owl hooted the age-old unanswered question. At a higher pitch, a coyote howled, perhaps in reaction to a barely gibbous moon. Stone stripped down to his briefs, weaved his clothing into a makeshift pillow, and slipped into the sleeping bag. He imagined that Bonnie was there with him. They were so very seldom apart on their married-life adventure. Finally, the sole camp sound was Stone's famous deep-throat snore. Stewart had brought ear plugs.

5

JIGGLIN' JUG RECON

Sunrise Tuesday:

They didn't bother with hot food for breakfast. Just drank fruit juice, chewed on chocolate chip cookies that Bonnie had made for the trip, and granola bars. Hardly a balanced meal, but sufficiently caloric to fuel them until lunchtime.

No clouds again, like yesterday. And it would get hot as the sun rose higher in the sky. They filled canteens, packed simple lunches, and broke camp by putting everything else into the truck. Backpacks in place, Stone locked that rig, and they set out by eight o'clock.

"Okay, great leader," Stone said. "Take me to your jug."

"Just follow me," Stewart replied.

Hiking was flat and easy for the first few yards from camp. Then they climbed onto the Little Springs lava flow, marked by an instant change from pine forest to barren black rock. The flow was about thirty feet thick. The flattish surface was what Hawaiians describe as between *pahoehoe* — a smooth, commonly ropy surface — and a broken tumbled lava top called *aa*. During his Kilauea years, Stone and colleagues there had coined a term for a lava-surface that is a mixture of these two. *Semihoe.* That description fit Little Springs. Easy walking for a few steps, followed by easy-to-stumble-on loose, spiny fragments. Repeatedly.

As they mounted the flow, Stone rolled down the sleeves of his shirt and donned a pair of leather gloves. He was wearing Red Wing boots, heavy leather high-top foot cover for lava walking. Stewart was barehanded, had his shirtsleeves rolled up, and was sporting his favorite jogging Nikes.

A several-hundred-foot-tall hill loomed three hundred yards ahead. Stewart pointed. "We buried the jug over there by the north base of the cinder cone. There's some solid ground for a sure contact with the jug to record whatever ground shaking might happen."

"Okay, let's go take a peek," Stone said, trudging forward.

Older and experienced with *semihoe*, Stone never stumbled. Meanwhile, Stewart lost his balance twice, cutting the fingers he used to cushion the falls. Somehow, he managed to not audibly take his lord's name in vain as he applied bandages.

"Dick," Stone said, in a somewhat condescending tone. "Here's a suggestion. At Kilauea we wear gloves to avoid those kinds of cuts. I brought some for ya."

Stone pulled a pair from his pack. Stewart put them on, with a quiet "thanks."

"The less exposed skin, the less risk of a nasty cut," Stone added.

Stewart lowered and buttoned his shirtsleeves. They walked on to the jug site.

Stewart and his technician had dug a shallow hole for the seismometer installation. Stone brushed away accumulated dust and pine needles, exposing the sturdy lid to an instrument cage that was solidly connected to the ground.

"Looks good to me," Stone observed. "That instrument shouldn't pick up small surface-caused trembles. They'd get damped out. But it should connect with deep-seated bedrock shaking."

"That's why we put it here," Stewart said. "And as I mentioned earlier, we thought that being so close to Little Springs Volcano might record a few shudders because it's so young — maybe has roots still cooling and shrinking."

"Okay, could happen, I guess," Stone agreed. "Let's look around on the lava flow."

They spent three hours traversing up and down and across the mile-long *semihoe* surface. Stone wanted to review evidence that magma had risen to the surface via a long north-south vertical fissure. Most had erupted at one spot to build the tall cinder cone. But at other nearby locations north and south of that hill, mini cones attested to local leaks of magma from at least several hundred yards of fissure. That showed up as a heavy dashed line on the map he and George had made. If that crack had propagated much further to the south, the odds of lava reaching and spilling into the Grand Canyon increased. *Maybe next time*, Stone mused.

While crisscrossing the *semihoe*, they also intersected obvious human-created pathways that had been smoothed across patches of *aa*. Several chest-high walls of stacked loose rock also decorated the lava surface. Once archaeologists had come to realize that the eruption had been observed by Native Americans, they painstakingly canvassed the flow surface for evidence of immediate-post-eruption human presence. Their current prevailing theory for the paths and walls was that the builders, Tribe A, retreated to these fortifications whenever Tribe B invaded their territory. *Another example of the age-old truth that Homo sapiens have a difficult time coexisting peacefully with each other*, Stone reminded himself. *And it seems there's nothing any god has been able to do about that.*

At noon, Stone and Stewart found a comfortable patch of *pahoehoe*, sat and consumed lunches washed down with by-now warm water. Stone noticed that Stewart's left-foot Nike had a long tear, insole side. *There goes a hundred bucks that could have been used to buy Red Wing boots*, he mused. *I'll let him figure that truth out for himself.*

Between chews on a leathery stick of dried meat, Stone said, "I'm now pretty well convinced those seismograms you showed me back at the office are recordings of ground shaking triggered by something beneath the surface."

Stewart smiled and nodded his approval of that thought.

"We've spent enough time here on the *semihoe*," Stone said. "Let's get off this rough stuff and drive down to the park ranger's house. Maybe he can add some useful information."

"Sounds good to me," Stewart chirped through a smile. "Let's go!" Stewart was feeling increasingly upbeat about the possibility that his seismic network was going to provide a strong case for continuation of his program and job at the university. *Even politicians should appreciate the value of watching for evidence that a new volcano might somehow harm the state's most famous attraction by damaging that huge moneymaker called the Grand Canyon. Job security means family security, means Sarah and I could proceed with our wish to bless the family with another child.*

6

THROWBACK RANGER

At 3 PM they pulled into the Toroweap Ranger Station of Grand Canyon National Park. There was the requisite entry sign "Welcome to Grand Canyon National Park, Toroweap" atilt on a weathered four-by-four post. A box screwed to the post contained brochures describing two available campsites that were further down the road. A weathered plywood-sided shed in need of paint — topped with a corrugated metal roof that fed into a gutter that drained into a large water storage tank — presumably contained whatever tools and equipment were needed at this outpost. Ranger housing was a rectangular cabin in a bit better condition than the shed. A large white propane tank was positioned a safe one hundred feet to one side. A lean-to off that side of the house sheltered a propane-fueled generator. A new, shiny-green Ranger pickup truck was parked out front. It looked out of place.

A sign hung by a nail on the entry door said "Knock loud. If no answer, I'm probably down at the campsites doing maintenance work."

Stone knocked, which set a dog to barking. Seconds later the door opened to expose what struck Stone as a scene out of the 1960s. The ranger wore an official National Park Service shirt, but beyond that he could have passed for a San Francisco hippie. Five-foot-ten, lean — almost emaciated looking. Long, oily hair was tied in a pony tail. A shaggy gray beard hung from weathered and wrinkled skin of a color that nearly matched the beard. Sandals appeared at the end of soiled denim jean pant legs. A healthy-looking adult male Doberman seemed incongruous.

"The National Park Service and I welcome you to Toroweap — called Tuweep by some," said the ranger in drawn-out cadence. The dog crotch-sniffed the new scents. "Rolf is friendly. He's my bosom buddy. I'm Mark. The lone ranger here."

He shook hands with Stone and Stewart while talking. Stewart kept the handshake as brief as politely possible. Stone pumped the proffered hand as though he and Mark were old pals.

"What can I do for you today, gentlemen?" Mark asked.

Stone took control. "I'm Franklin Stone, and this is Richard Stewart. We're geology professors from Northern Arizona University in Flagstaff."

"So pleased to meet ya, professors," Mark drawled. "I get down to your town once or twice a year for supplies I can't find in Fredonia. Nice lookin' campus ya got there at NAU."

"Thanks," Stone replied. "It's summer break now, and we're up here to look at some of the volcanoes in your backyard. I was here a few years ago with another geologist, mappin' those volcanoes. There was a different ranger back then. A guy named Kent, I think."

"Ya, Kent, that's right," Mark said, after a moment of apparent thought. "I'm his replacement. Kent kinda fled almost two years ago. Couldn't stand the isolation."

Stone knew that Toroweap had a history of frequent turnover for ranger duty, specifically because of the isolation. Young people got bored. Old people got worried. Singles tended to last longer than married couples. Whatever the situation, one to two years was about the maximum stay.

"But me, I like it here," Mark added. "Just me, Rolf, Bertha, and Finney get along fine. We don't need, or want the trimmin's that most folks seem to."

"Well, we don't want to disturb your mellow setup," said Stone, changing the subject. "But here's what we came to ask about." Stone motioned toward Stewart. "Dick here is a seismologist."

That long, unfamiliar word set Mark to tugging on his beard.

"You know," Stone explained. "One of those guys who study earthquakes."

"Ah. Sure, got it," Mark said. "I used to live in California — land of shake and break. So what are you doin' in mellow old northern Arizona? Life's been a smooth and quiet trip for as long as I've lived here."

"Well, here's the thing," Stone replied. "Dick has a seismometer station just outside the park, near Little Springs. It's been there several years. Quiet and mellow, like you say. But recently, for the first time ever, it's been recording what we think are small earthquakes."

"Really?" Mark said with obvious interest. "Sounds kinda fascinating. I wanna hear about this. Let's go inside — sit down there and get comfy so you can continue your yarn."

Mark swung the door wide, and they entered. Half walls at the ends of the rectangular floor plan separated a small kitchen and a toilet/bedroom from the central living room. Two folding chairs, a threadbare couch, and a small weathered-wood table occupied that space. A two-gallon clear-glass bowl with a goldfish sat on the table. An overweight black cat was asleep against one arm of the sofa. Two windows in the south-facing wall let in enough sunlight to read on cloud-free days.

"Meet Bertha and Finney," Mark said, gesturing toward the cat and fishbowl. "Grab a seat and tell me more about this earthquake thing."

Stone and Stewart took the chairs. Mark plopped down on the couch, next to an already comfortably ensconced Rolf, who moved his head to Mark's lap.

Stewart remained silent. His body language shouted *Let's leave.* The space smelled of unwashed things, decaying foods, and hard to tell what else. The walls were decorated with clippings from publications foreign to him. The pages had lots of blazing colors in random contorted patterns. Stone just grinned and continued to talk.

"Actually, we're kinda hopin' you might be able to tell us about earthquakes," Stone said. "Your place here is only a few miles from Dick's instrument. Maybe you've felt some vibrations? Like when you were sittin' still and felt a strange jiggle?"

"Nope," Mark answered. "Nothin' like that. It's been quiet and dreamy out here. Just me, the animals, music, food, drink, and my evening pipe."

"What about Rolf and Bertha?" Stone asked. "Any unusual behavior?"

Stone's mind had flashed back to his early career years at Kilauea. During high fountains of lava that came with most eruptions then, the nearby ground shook enough that people close in could feel a rhythmic sway. Further out, where people felt nothing unusual, the family dog that he and Bonnie kept would regularly slip into fits of fear-filled trembling.

Their family cat slept through it all. *In fact their cat napped most of its life*, Stone recalled as he looked at a sleeping Bertha.

Mark again pulled at his beard, apparently probing his memory, and said. "I guess nothin' could disturb Bertha. She's a typical house cat. Sleeps most of the time, and moves around just enough to process some food and water on its way to the sand box."

Stewart could see and smell that box, sitting under a porcelain sink in the sleeping quarters. He was ready to wrap up their visit and get out of this dingy place. He defensively kept his legs and arms tightly crossed.

Mark's eyes brightened a bit. "Now that you bring it up, though, for some reason Rolf has been an off-again, on-again eater for the past several months. He's gettin' old for a Dobie. Ten last January. Hindquarters are arthritic. A vet in Fredonia sells me pain pills for that. They do the trick. I hide those in with his regular food and down the hatch they go. Twice a day."

Hearing his name, Rolf licked Mark's hand and paused for a scratch behind his ears.

Mark continued. "There've been days, though, when he wouldn't touch his food. Or even his pill when I tried to feed it to him by hand. He'd just tremble, bark and growl a bit, and then retreat to his cushion. He was feelin' some pain, I figured. I couldn't see anything threatening that might be botherin' him. It's like, ya know, people have bad days from time to time, too."

He pulled his ponytail to one side and leaned back on the sofa. "There was nothin' regular about that behavior, though. Just seemed to come and go kinda random like. He always got back on his feedbag. Never really lost any weight."

Mark paused, lost in some bit of recollection, while rubbing Rolf's ears. "I kept real close track of those times. Thought my vet might be able to see some pattern to help with treatment. Me and Rolf are like brothers, ya know. I look after him. And he looks after me. Don't have any other family. Rolf and I are about as bonded as a dog and a man can be."

Stone nodded in acknowledgement. He, too, now wanted fresh air. He stood to go. "Well, thanks for your thoughts and hospitality. We'll be on our way. We're gonna spend tonight down at the campground near Vulcan's Throne. If you're up early tomorrow, you'll see us drive out."

Mark and Rolf walked out to the NAU truck with Stone and Stewart. More handshakes, this time in farewell. Stewart took the passenger seat. Stone had a brief last-minute exchange with Mark before sliding behind the steering wheel. Rolf was busy, with lifted leg, peeing on a hubcap.

"Sure, Dr. Stone. I'll do my best to take care of that tonight," Mark said as the NAU's diesel engine barked to life. "Now don't you two guys have a wild late nighter and roll off that three-thousand-foot cliff."

No chance of that, Frank mused as they drove away, southward toward the campsites.

"Did you get anything useful from that conversation?" Stewart asked, as they bounced along the roughest stretch of road at Toroweap.

"No, not really," Stone answered. "Other than there's an old sixties-style hippie or two still around. I doubt that Mark would be able to tell an earth shake from a ganja tremble, unless his house was fallin' down around him. Seems the well-dressed, clean-shaven rangers at the South Rim are hired under stricter standards than those for Toroweap. But hey. Somebody's got to maintain this outpost."

Stewart nodded and made a mental note to look up the meaning of ganja.

There were two campgrounds at Toroweap. One sat well back from the lip of the Grand Canyon, at the base of tall cliffs eroded in colorful, horizontal sedimentary rocks. Stone had little use for this geology, other than imaging it as a layer cake waiting for black chocolaty lava frosting.

The other site sat on the brink of the canyon. The views from there were mind-bending. A couple of stray volcanoes were visible to the south, straight across the canyon — stray in the sense that ninety-nine percent of their cousins were on the north side of the canyon, all snuggled around Little Springs, the baby of the lot. A peer down into the canyon revealed Lava Falls Rapid, described as the most challenging in the Grand Canyon by professional river runners. And the three-thousand-foot drop from rim to river was about as close to vertical as one could imagine. For some reason, the national park had never constructed a guard railing. The Toroweap ranger advised overnight visitors with a penchant to sleepwalk to stay at the "inland" campsite.

Tired from the day's activities, Stone and Stewart nibbled on cold food; no campfire tonight. And neither wanted to set up the propane stove.

Stewart then slipped into the tent and continued reading, just as he had the previous night.

Stone stayed awake to enjoy the night sky in complete darkness — other than a wee bit of moonshine, and the faint glow of Stewart's light diffused by tent fabric. Stone moved far enough from the tent to avoid that distraction. A clear night view of the sky was almost magical when away from any artificial lighting.

An hour later, having identified as many constellations as he could remember from his college astronomy course, Stone wished a mental, *Goodnight lover,* to Bonnie. He could faintly hear the sound of water cascading through the rapid below. Stripped down to his shorts, he slipped into his sleeping bag and gazed at a yellow, gibbous shape until his eyelids slammed shut. Then the snoring began.

1

CORRELATION! CAUSE AND EFFECT?

Wednesday:

They broke camp at dawn, chewed on more cold food, packed up and drove away. Both, for different reasons, were anxious to get back to Flagstaff and the comforts of home. Stone could see that Stewart was an office kind of geologist, not a field person. No surprise there. Stone craved fieldwork, to the point that his left knee gave out after years of bedrock scrambling. He missed not having with Bonnie on this adventure. She had accompanied him on so many of his fieldwork stints.

Stone drove, feeling certain that Stewart would damage the truck, if not its passengers, by navigating as though a rough eroded bedrock surface was smoothed, packed-down asphalt. He pulled in at Ranger Mark's house and found a folded sheet of paper, tacked to the cabin door. He read the message silently to himself. "The enclosed dates are the times when Rolf went off his normal feed, as best I can reconstruct them. Some of the notes I kept on scraps of paper were blurred. I think I got most of the info though. Maybe even all of it. Hope this is of use. I'm off to Fredonia for supplies. Mark"

"What's up?" Stewart asked.

"Nothin' important," Stone said as he tucked the note into his backpack. He wasn't yet ready to share his notion that animal behavior might help in the search for an explanation to the still-mysterious jiggles of Stewart's jug. "Mark's just lettin' us know why he's not here this morning. We may see him or his truck in Fredonia."

They did see that truck at a grocery store, as they drove through town. A large black canine head with pointed ears and tan eyebrows hung out the passenger window, right above a vertical trail of drool that decorated the door. And they did once again stop at the visitor center at the west end of Navajo Bridge, to drain human-processed fluids. But mostly, Stone just drove about ten miles an hour above the speed limit. Stewart complained about not sleeping well both nights; he blamed that lack of sleep on hard ground and Stone's snoring, which penetrated his earplugs. He promised himself to upgrade before another camp-out with Stone. After Rainbow Bridge, he slept, lying across the backseat.

Stone woke him as he pulled into his home driveway, mid-afternoon. Bonnie appeared at the front entry moments after the horn honk. The garage door was on its way up. She and Stone met and hugged and kissed, Bonnie standing on the middle step of the stoop. She helped her man unload his gear. Stewart was now on his feet, slipping behind the steering wheel while yawning — loudly.

"Let's meet at my office tomorrow morning," Stone suggested, "if you can get going by then. I'm about ready to tell you what I think's happenin' with that shakin' jug of yours."

"Okay," Stewart agreed. "How about no earlier than ten, so I can spend more time with my wife and kids." This carried the tone of a declarative statement, not a question. *Pretty strong stuff for mister puffball,* Stone mused.

"Fine with me," Stone said. "I'd like a little extra quality home time, too. See you tomorrow. Bring those seismograms with you." Stewart nodded and drove away.

Bonnie pulled Stone into a far corner of the garage, out of view for any passersby. "I've got a rack of pork ribs, three-bean salad, and cold beer planned for dinner," she said. "Afternoon BBQ delight. How's that sound?"

"Yummy," Stone cooed. "But first I want to spend time with somethin' important I brought back from Toroweap. If I don't do this now, I won't be ready for the rendezvous with Stewart tomorrow."

"Okay, I guess," Bonnie said. "I need to do a slow tenderizing of the ribs at low heat anyway. So they'll melt in our mouths after you grill them."

Stone reached down to find Ranger Mark's note in the backpack. "Perfect menu, lover," he said, somewhat absentmindedly.

Bonnie pulled him back to face her. "Come here," she commanded, as she looped her arms around his neck. "How about an hors d'oeuvre?" she added as she closed any space between them.

Stone recognized this welcome command from his life partner. He dropped the note. His hands cupped Bonnie's firm buttocks as they shared a lingering wet kiss. She was hangin' on tight around his shoulders, feet barely touching the floor. They came up for air.

"That's better," she said. "I was starting to wonder if you'd forgotten how you should greet me after being away so long," she added. "By the way, did you happen to bring one of those rock-hard samples back in your jeans again? Seems you do most every time you come home from one of your spouse-free field trips," Bonnie said, through a wide grin.

Stone nodded as he created a bit of space between them and gazed down. "Well, by gosh, looky there," he said, and quickly added as they returned to the full-body clinch, "I sure hope we never grow up. Being adult would be so boring." Their laughter filled the garage space.

Bonnie headed to the kitchen to get the rib tenderizing under way. Stone disappeared into his home office and sat at his antique oak rolltop desk.

He looked over the information that accompanied Mark's note to see how long and complete a record he had compiled about Rolf's fits of trembling and going off his feed. A calendar year, more or less. He reached to the right, opened a sliding drawer, and extracted a sheet of graph paper from a file. This was anachronistic stuff to his university colleagues. They would be looking at the same square grid pattern on the monitor screen of a PC or Mac.

He inked two black lines at right angles to each other, meeting at a point near the lower left corner of the sheet. Then he labeled equal lengths of the lines from zero to four hundred, by increments of twenty, to represent a bit more than a year of days. Parallel to and under the horizontal line he wrote Rolf. The vertical became Jiggles.

He plotted the info from the Rolf file as vertical lines spaced according to the dates in Mark's notes. One bad day for Rolf was a thin line. Multiple successive days were appropriately thicker. The data spanned from about mid May of a year ago to just last week.

Information for Jiggles came from a compilation Stewart had provided before their field trip. It went back further in time than the info about Rolf's eating disorder. Stone found the oldest occurrence of time overlap and plotted horizontal lines for periods of jug jiggle from there on to the present. Thin lines represented twenty-four hours or less of jiggle. And as with Rolf lines, they were thicker in proportion with the duration of continuous jiggling beyond a day. A clear pattern emerged.

"Bonnie!" Stone shouted. "Come here! Zounds, my wifely Shakespeare! Hurry!"

She appeared, bearing his usual predinner Cuba libre and her partly consumed gin and tonic.

"Here I am," she said, handing Stone his drink. "Now, what's so exciting that I had to leave the kitchen?"

"Look at this," Stone gushed, holding out the Rolf-versus-Jiggles graph.

Their conversation morphed into the kind of mental game they had played out many times during Stone's volcano career, times when he got super excited about some of his research. Or times when she feigned near boredom with his enthusiasm. And then later used Stone's discovery as the basis for another travel story to sell.

Bonnie grabbed the sheet of graph paper and took a quick glance at what Stone had inked in.

"What's the big deal?" she asked. "I've seen an X versus Y plot before. And this one's pretty sloppy. Look at those thick lines. Was your hand shaky? Did you use one of those so-called Sharpies instead of a fine-tipped pen for them? Why do that? And what's with the boxes of various sizes where lines cross?"

Stone interrupted. "Hey! Look at the big picture." He was semi-serious now. "Forget the width of lines and sizes of boxes. Just mentally connect the crossings. There's a linear pattern slanting upward at forty-five degrees."

Bonnie feigned another studious examination of the graph. "Am I supposed to be impressed or surprised?" she asked.

"Bonnie, don't you see?" Stone shouted. "Rolf and Jiggles are in a straight relationship! I've caught them in the act. And I'm gonna use that info as a lever to my advantage to help explain what's been goin' on at Toroweap."

Stone stood. They held hands facing each other. Without saying another word, they both realized that he now had a new entry for his bucket list. And that she wouldn't have to verbally council him out of his recent moodiness. He was in full smile, something that had been missing for too long. She was mentally outlining a new story.

"Let's feast on those ribs and trimmings," he said. "Then, I propose a long wine-sipping soak in the hot tub, followed by creating jiggles in the bladder of our water bed."

"Thought you'd never suggest!" Bonnie crooned, in sync with a slow wink.

8

AWKWARD COLLABORATION

Thursday 6 AM:

Stone and Bonnie woke, entwined in each other's arms, to a mellifluous voice reading national and local news on NPR affiliate KNAU. A cranky voice would have been more in keeping with the stories. The Middle East was still in religious/political turmoil. Nationally, functioning political parties in the U. S. continued to fight over what the word compromise means in practice. No resolution seemed forthcoming.

Locally, Flagstaff's city government continued to pursue its decades-long feasibility study of how to procure and assure an adequate future potable water supply. There was barely enough supply for current demand. Surface water was virtually nonexistent in the drought-plagued climate, and drilling additional wells near town was incredibly expensive. During the past decade, depth to the water table had increased from two thousand to nearly three thousand feet. The current favorite plan was to purchase yet more land, and rights to its subterranean water resource, far to the east of town, and to pump that liquid uphill to a thirsty populace. A huge fiscal bond would be required. The search for more water, either increasingly downward or eastward, was likely to "break the bank."

Stone had been part of the city's water-feasibility-study team during several of the two-thousand-teen years, volunteering his geologic experience and perspectives to city managers who didn't seem to understand that, yes, a volume of water can be safely reused for human consumption if appropriately reclaimed. Those managers operated on the basis that people could never again safely imbibe once-used potable water.

Stone had eventually stormed out of a meeting, shouting, "If everyone operated with that attitude, there would soon be no safely potable water anywhere on planet Earth. Next thing you idiots will dream up is that once-breathed air is permanently contaminated! And there's damned little air here at seven thousand feet elevation to begin with. Bah! I give up! I quit!"

This morning, he was thinking that he and Stewart would have to find some way to work together smoothly, with compromise where necessary because of their very real differences, personally and professionally. He silently swore to himself that he would not storm out of this morning's meeting.

Stone and Bonnie showered together, toweled off, and then donned terry-cloth robes. The words TREASURE CHEST were embroidered across the front of Bonnie's. Stone's read OPEN FOR BUSINESS. College classmates had given them the original set of robes as wedding gifts. Stone and Bonnie kept this and other pleasant college memories alive by purchasing new robes as old ones became too threadbare for continued use.

They walked to the kitchen for breakfast, opening curtains for the view of surrounding pine forest. The sun was low to the east, in a cloud-free sky. Birds were singing and some of their annual flowers were in full bloom. It looked as though their lone lilac bush would even crank out a few flowers this year.

Stone ate a breakfast of hash browns, two over-easy eggs, crisp-fried bacon, jam-slathered toast, orange juice, and strong coffee. More of everything than usual. He was making up for eating so simply during the trip to Toroweap. Bonnie ate a cup of cherry-flavored yogurt. Hunger satisfied, Stone brushed his teeth, shaved, replaced his robe with blue jeans and a tee-shirt, and stuffed papers and such including the Jiggles/Rolf graph into his backpack along with a full lunch bucket. He kissed Bonnie goodbye at the door.

"What's on your agenda today, lover?" he asked.

Bonnie smiled. "Yoga class at nine. And then I plan to work on a story for *Travel and Pleasure Magazine*. It's due in a week, and I'm still trying to figure out how to create a happy ending for an Alaskan fjords cruise that so often is socked in with fog and rain. But I'll figure something out, because it's important to me."

She reached out and took his hands in hers. "I'm sure you'll find a way to work it out with Stewart, too. I know that's important to you."

"Is it that obvious?" Stone asked, feigning surprise.

"Yes," she said. "So just do it!"

"Well, here I go," Stone snapped, executing a rigid military-style salute as he spoke. They smiled together, and parted with a hand squeeze. Stone marched down the entryway steps and began his walk to NAU. *I'm sure she could see right through my most inner soul, even if I wore lead-lined clothes.* Without immediately realizing so, he found himself humming the lyrics to "Happy Days are Here Again."

*   *   *

Stewart was waiting at Stone's office door, looking neat and perky, steaming cup of tea in hand. Stone noticed new Nikes, wear and tear free.

"Good morning, Franklin," Stewart greeted.

Stone nodded and keyed the lock. "Come on in," he invited. He closed the door behind Stewart. Today, Stone preferred privacy. He didn't want their discussion interrupted in mid stream, before some acceptable working relationship was agreed to. "Have a seat."

Stewart did. Then Stone sat and swiveled his chair so they were facing each other, about six feet apart. No office coffee for him today; he'd had plenty with breakfast. A bit of awkward silence ensued as each seemed to maneuver for maximum comfort in his chair.

Finally, Stone broke the still. "Before we get into the science of what's goin' on at Toroweap," he began, "I want to establish our working relationship."

Stone looked down at the ratty floor tiles, and then continued. "We're pretty much at opposite ends of the spectrum on social, political, religious, and even some scientific issues."

Stewart nodded, in apparent agreement.

"In all honesty," Stone added, "I probably would never have invited you to be a coworker on a project of mine, because of our differences. Wouldn't be surprised if you felt the same way about collaboratin' with me."

Stewart nodded, again.

Stone pressed on. "But it seems that chance and Nature have put us on the same team for the first time. And I think the game is way too important to suffer for strictly personal differences."

Stewart gave another quick curt nod — his face bearing a blank neutral expression.

"Okay," Stone said. "So I say we go forward with one caveat: Beliefs that come with your religion will not be any part of our collaboration. Not at all!"

A fourth nod.

To further emphasize his point, Stone said, "Believe whatever you want in your private life, but you and I are going to be talkin' and writin' about events that trash your Bible's clock for the geology of Toroweap and the Grand Canyon."

Stewart finally spoke. "Yes, yes," he affirmed. "That's fine with me. Let's just get to the science."

That was too easy, Stone thought. *I guess he's super worried about losing his NAU job, with such a large and growing family to support. That reason works for me if it works for him.*

What had been palpable about-to-burst stretched-balloon tension in the air, leaked quietly away.

"Okay then," Stone switched gears. "Let's start with the short version of what I think is goin' on with your jigglin' jug."

Stone extended his right fist toward Stewart and began with an unfurled index finger. "Number one: I'm totally convinced that your seismograms result from natural tremblin' caused by something happenin' down in Earth."

"Number two." Stone now extended his second finger, pointed at Stewart. "Those records are like ones of seismic shakin' at Kilauea. They've been recorded there many times since the 1950s. That's when seismic jugs were first installed across the volcano. Lots of jugs recording the same thing at the same time."

Stone might as well have been talking to a wall — or so it seemed. Stewart sat motionless with an unchanging enigmatic facial expression. His tea had gone cold, with his cup still full.

Stone's point number three brought his ring finger into play. "This shakin' at Kilauea is called harmonic tremor," he said. "It's caused by fluid forcibly risin' up through cracks in Earth's crust."

A hint of a smile developed across Stewart's face.

"Number four," said Stone, adding his pinkie to the digit count. "And this should give *you* a tremor. Harmonic tremor hits right before eruptions at Kilauea. To put it plain and simple, in not too much of a generalization: It's magma on the rise!"

Stewart leaped up from his dwindling stupor, with fisted right hand raised high, cold tea splashing across the tiles of the office floor. "Glory be!" he shouted. "Yes! Yes! I thought that's what has been happening at Toroweap, from what I've read about Kilauea. But I wanted to hear it from someone with hands-on experience."

Stone found Stewart's childish enthusiasm a bit entertaining. "Easy there Dick," he said. "Don't burst an artery."

Stewart sat, quietly.

"And watch your language," Stone added. "Remember what you agreed to a couple minutes ago?"

"Yes. Sorry," Stewart murmured. "What's next? What should we do now?"

"I've got a plan," Stone said. "But first, let's take a pee break. I had too much coffee for breakfast."

9

A PROJECT TAKES SHAPE

Later Thursday AM:

Stone and Stewart met back in Stone's office. Stone began to explain his plan.

"With your seismograms," he said, "we've got a good start on the science of what's happenin' at Toroweap. Those records are key to developing our story. But we need to get more jugs in the volcano area so we can pinpoint the surface spot that magma seems headed toward. I doubt you'll be able to get your project budget and personnel increased to do this. But I've got a backup plan."

Stewart listened attentively.

"Through contacts at my old employer the USGS," Stone continued, "I might be able to get colleagues there to help us. I'll look into that ASAP."

"But what should we be doing here, right now?" Stewart asked.

"We've already got enough info, to start spreadin' the word to university colleagues," Stone said. "The annual meeting of the Southwestern Geological Society is coming up in Tucson soon. We should submit papers for back-to-back talks there. You can lead off with your jigglin' jug story. I'll follow with a comparison to Kilauea."

"I thought you might suggest that," Stewart said. "I've already got a draft of my findings worked up for you to critique."

"Good!" Stone acknowledged. "I'll start writing my piece later today."
Maybe this religious zealot and I have more in common than I've been thinking.

Stone thought for a moment in silence, with a worried expression on his face. "Then there's the politics. Never thought I'd care about this kind of crap, but we can't ignore it. We're gonna propose the possibility of another eruption at Toroweap. An eruption that could whack the Grand Canyon. And even though we don't know for sure what's gonna happen, we'll probably be branded by some as scaremongers. Nothin' compared to the folks who from time to time say that Earth may be destroyed by the impact of a big asteroid. But still, the idea that eruption might mess up the Grand Canyon will raise hackles. Especially 'cause there's the well-known history of prehistoric lava dams and the havoc they wreaked up- and down-stream."

Stewart listened quietly. *I've had the same thoughts about the politics of what we're into. Best to let Franklin lead for now.*

"Let's describe the situation to our department chair, Crystal Bond," Stone suggested. "Then she can work up the administrative ladder, eventually to the NAU President, who can reach out to the other state university presidents. Then I guess it's on up to the University Board of Regents, et cetera et cetera. Man! I can't believe I'm saying this stuff. I hate politics!"

"But you're right, Franklin," Stewart said. "We can't avoid this, given the story we're going to tell."

He paused and scanned Stone, top to bottom, and then added, "You might want to consider dressing up a bit when we need to put on a convincing public face."

"Bullshit!" growled Stone. "If somebody doesn't like the way I look that's their problem."

In a calmer voice, Stone continued, "You contact Crystal and set up a meeting with her for tomorrow morning. Meanwhile, e-mail me your abstract. I'll have mine ready to send to you by the end of the day."

Friday AM:

Stone and Stewart met with Crystal, who was excited both by the science and by the opportunities this could bring to her department. She promised to move this quickly up the administrative ladder.

By the end of the workday, the Toroweap team had finalized their abstracts and emailed them to SWGS Headquarters for approval and scheduling for oral presentation at the upcoming meeting in Tucson.

That Evening:

Spirits were high in the Stone household. Bonnie had successfully created a fun-in-the-fog ending for her travel story and sent that file to her editor. Stone was giddy with what he called the Toroweap Two-Step. They celebrated the weekend by driving down Oak Creek Canyon to Sedona, where they dined, window-shopped, and watched tourists. They returned to Flagstaff once again wondering if the tourist-infested city of Sedona was real, with permanent home-owning residents. Or was it simply a movie set where ephemeral casts played out dramas in unending succession, featuring pink Jeeps, magical quartz crystals, spiritual stone circles, and soul-cleansing sweat lodges.

10

VOLCANO SWAT TEAM

Monday AM:

At his NAU office desk, Stone punched the phone number for the USGS Cascades Volcano Observatory in Vancouver, Washington. A familiar cheery female voice answered with "U.S. Geological Survey. How can I help you?"

"Hi Lois," Stone said. "Well, my friend, you could start by not soundin' so damned professional and wide awake early on a Monday morning."

"Frank?" she responded. "Franklin Stone that must be you, you old rogue."

Her tone of voice changed from question to declarative-statement mode without missing a beat.

"I haven't heard from or about you for months and months — not since you left the USGS and became a hoity-toity professor," she said.

"No hoity or toity, Lois," Stone said. "It's the same old curmudgeon me, just answerin' to a different boss. Actually, I don't really have a boss here at NAU. Just a comfortable platform for workin' on projects the USGS thought were too academic for their standards. I love it here."

Stone heard Lois say good morning, presumably to a USGS employee arriving for another day of chasing volcanoes.

"So Lois, how's your life movin' along?" Stone asked. "Still married to that goofy vintner who produces some of Washington's best whites?"

"Yup," Lois replied. "And that goofy vintner is winning competitions with his pinot grigio. Why don't you buy a case or two or ten? Then maybe

I could retire early and join him in the annual wine cycle. The vines are just starting to show new growth. Getting ready for another bumper crop, we hope.

"How's Bonnie doing?" Lois continued, after a brief pause. "I suppose *she* has to keep working, too, so you can play around in academia."

"Oh, you smarty-pants," Stone joked. "You see right through us self-centered guys, don't ya!"

"Well, she's still crankin' out the travel stories, in spite of the fact that my project travellin' days are pretty much over as a source of new ideas for her," Stone said.

"What do you mean *over*?" Lois asked. "Franklin Stone and volcano-climbing are pretty much synonymous in geology circles."

"Yes, but titanium steel rubbin' against patella ain't pleasant while scramblin' up a mountainside," Stone explained.

"New knee, huh?" Lois said. "We're all getting older and slowing down a bit, aren't we. So, what prompted you to call up the nation's second citadel of volcano studies today?"

"Believe it or not," Stone said, lowering his voice, "I think I've got one more big volcano project stirrin' in my old bones. One that doesn't call for a lot of walkin'. I need to talk with Dan Baker about it. Is he in today?"

"I saw him walk down the hall toward his office a few minutes ago," Lois said. "I'll connect you.

"And, hey. Good to talk with you. Give Bonnie a hug for me."

"Sure," Stone said. "You know I love any excuse to give her an extra hug. Say hi to Josh for me. And tell him to keep on fermentin' and bottlin'. I sometimes wish the fluid of my career was as tasty as his."

When Washington State's Mount St. Helens erupted violently in 1980, the USGS quickly established its second volcano observatory, nearby in Vancouver, and named it the Cascade Volcano Observatory. Most folks of the startup CVO staff were on temporary assignment from HVO at Kilauea. As an ex-HVOer, Stone had been temporarily uprooted from his Arizona post to join the makeshift CVO group tending to Mount St. Helens. And he'd kept in touch with the permanent Cascades staff ever since. There was nothing like working together on a violent eruption in the lower forty-eight for promoting professional bonding. Stone and Baker were prime evidence of that truism.

"Frank! How the H are you?" Baker bellowed. "It's been way too long since our trails last crossed."

Dan Baker had the self-assured commanding voice of someone in charge — like a ship's captain or a plane's pilot. In fact, Dan was a plane nut, always rebuilding old biwing things or assembling state-of-the-art two-passenger aircraft from kits. That thought made Stone feel a bit queasy by remembering the one, and only, sustained inverted flight of his life. It had been with Baker, over the newly blasted-out crater of Mount St. Helens. What a view, from upside down! He captured some spectacular photos that day. The plane was a tandem-seat, open-cockpit WWI-vintage something-or-other from Spain that Baker had rebuilt to current safety specifications. Not trusting his seat belt, Stone had held on to metal side panels like a scared kid when they were upside down. It terrified him, yet in a pleasantly exciting way, if such is possible. Unforgettable!

"Agreed, my friend," Stone said. "If my memory hasn't totally failed, I think we last met face-to-face in the Manila airport back in 1991. You were returnin' to the U.S. mainland from the Pinatubo Volcano disaster. I was on the way in for a month of helpin' to monitor the follow-up to that wild eruption."

"Yeah," Baker agreed. "That's the way I remember it, too. Lucky none of our crew died, huh? That was an unforgettable eruption experience — and not just the geology part."

"Yeah, I'll say," Stone reminisced. "Still seems ironic, doesn't it? Pinatubo drove the U.S. military presence out of the Philippines, after politics failed to do so. Like the coffee mug in my right hand says, Volcanoes Rule!" Stone took a loud slurp of Joe.

Silence spoke volumes of mental meanderings into the distant past at both ends of the phone link. Then ...

"Man, the time has flown since Pinatubo," Baker said. "You should come up here for a reunion before we no longer even recognize each other. Hell, just move up here where the real lower forty-eight volcanic action is. You must be pretty bored there in Grand Canyon country. We create new land, not erode it away to form a huge ditch."

"That's true to date, my friend," Stone said, getting to the reason for his call. "But here's a surprise for ya. I've phoned 'cause I think the next lower forty-eight eruption will be in my backyard, not yours. And I need some help to pin down what's actually goin' on here."

Baker was stunned. "Wait just a minute, Franklin. Are you serious? Or am I talking with the old leg-pulling guy?"

Stone summarized the evidence of tremor within the Uinkaret volcanic field, including a few words about his Mormon seismologist project partner.

"What we need now is a half dozen or so additional seismometers spread over the area to try to pinpoint the depth where shakin' originates," Stone explained. "And to figure out where that projects up to the ground surface. We need good three-D info. And I'm thinkin' this might be a perfect project for the VDAP team there at Vancouver. Even if we could get the money from the state down here, we don't have the trained people to get goin' and get goin' fast."

The Volcano Disaster Assistance Program of the USGS existed to help volcano geologists in foreign countries where tools of the trade and appropriately trained staff were in short supply. The Pinatubo project had been an early success in term of lives and property saved.

"I know Arizona ain't a needy foreign country," Stone said. "Though its politics come across that way too often for my tastes. But you guys at CVO have the instruments and know-how that we badly need right now!"

"And maybe if CVO did its VDAP business communications down here in Spanish, Navajo, and Hopi, the overseers could look the other way," Stone joked.

They mulled over some of the details of what was needed. Baker promised to do what he could to convince the VDAP team to help Stone and his seismologist partner in Flagstaff.

Tuesday AM:

Stone sat slouched over his office desk gazing at the Rolf-versus-Jiggles graph, trying to reason out when and where he should go public with the notion that the behavior of a pet Doberman might be an aide to hard science. He might be ridiculed by colleagues — and the public. *But, damn it, my personal experience at Kilauea says that Ranger Mark's Rolf is just another example of what a subtle earth tremor can elicit from a sensitive canine.*

His phone rang. "Frank Stone here," he said.

Before he could add the usual *what's on your mind?* a familiar voice said, "Good news, my friend. The VDAP team will work with you and Stewart at Toroweap." It was Baker.

"Fan-effin'-tastic!" Stone said, sitting upright. "How'd you get such fast results?"

"In a word, serendipity," Baker confided. "I could suggest that someone up there likes you, but I'll let you save that explanation for Stewart if you want to use an alternative to just plain unexpected good luck. The VDAP team has an entirely new generation of seismometers that they want to test in the field. And you, Doctor Stone, have the perfect setting for the test. A place that right now has the kind of seismic signal they want the new jugs to recognize and record. When do you want them down there? They're ready to go, the sooner the better. They have a pending request for help from folks in Chile, but want a shakedown cruise for the new jugs before going down there."

"How about later this week?" Stone suggested. "Weather's lookin' good for field work."

Baker agreed. "I'll have Norm, the VDAP lead guy, call so you two can work out a plan."

"Dan. I owe you big time, buddy," Stone said.

"Damn straight!" Baker responded. "And I won't let you forget it. Add a visit to CVO to your well-known bucket list. Bring Bonnie and we'll party. Lena and I have a big new hot tub. And I've got a new Spitfire X we can cruise the Cascades in. Maybe fly over St. Helens again."

"Deal!" Stone said. "I'd like that."

After a brief pause, he added. "As long as the flight isn't buttcrack to the sky."

Stone could hear the loud guffaws of Baker as he disconnected their phone link.

Wednesday thru Sunday:

Volcanologist Norm Wright and his crew of technicians flew into the Flagstaff airport Wednesday afternoon. Stone met them and helped load their equipment into two rental minivans. He guided them to the Little America Motel for the night. Then Stone drove home, where he found Bonnie typing the tale of a new *Bouncing* adventure.

Thursday morning, the VDAP crew caravanned with Stone and Stewart to Toroweap. By Sunday afternoon, eight new seismometers were in place in a pattern over the entire area of young volcanoes. One instrument was positioned next to Stewart's jigglin' jug, so recordings of the old and new could be compared as a control point. All nine instruments would beam their records in real time to the VDAP CVO office and to Stewart's office at NAU.

Before the crew left to return to Flagstaff, Stone learned from Ranger Mark that Rolf had once again gone briefly off his normal feed, two days earlier. *The same time that Stewart had reported another short episode of jiggle. One more point for the graph.*

11

SPREADING THE WORD

The Following Wednesday:

About midmorning, Chairlady Bond called Stone and Stewart to her office. Her long neatly combed blond hair hung halfway to her waist. Her skirt and blouse were in harmony with dress code for the day of the week. Only Stone looked sartorially out of place. He almost always did — in any setting. His tee-shirt today was emblazoned with "Geogolists Don't Know." He was forever pleased to explain the story behind the misspelling, if asked.

"Good morning, Frank and Richard," she said. "Have a seat."

Stone smiled and winked as he sat. She winked back. He and Bond shared a comfortable relationship. She was about Bonnie's size and with a similar easygoing personality. The main physical contrast was Bonnie's dark and naturally curly hair.

Bond's office included a comfortable sofa where Frank and Stewart sat at opposite ends, facing her perched behind her polished mahogany desk. She was leaning back in her chair, nearly hidden behind tall stacks of stuff filling boxes labeled In and Out. Digital files had not yet totally replaced their hard-copy forerunners.

"I've already reported your discovery of tremor bursts at Toroweap and the current interpretation of what that means to our NAU President," Bond said. "Based on that, she'll be presenting a case for a permanent and expanded seismic program for NAU when the three university presidents meet in Phoenix later this week. Her proposal will include a request to hire another seismologist, to share your current duties, Stewart."

The slap sound of Stone and Stewart high-fiving reverberated off the walls and windows. Bond smiled.

"So, we're under way on the university politics," she continued.

She leaned forward and pointed a wagging index finger toward the professors for emphasis. "Meanwhile, you two need to get the word out to your professional colleagues about the science," she said. "Stir the pot. Get some excitement going. Of course, eventually we're going to need a much stronger scientific case to support our wish to expand the department. I agree with your current interpretation of what's happening, but it's only a hypothesis. We need more data. More testing. Verification."

Bond leaned back again, to relax. "When we get into the Arizona politics of the situation, we have to convince the money managers that the value of knowing what's up with the Toroweap volcano area is a critical economic issue and an issue of public safety," she said. "It's got to be a lot more than pure science. Most of those elected officials are lawyers or business people, who don't know much science."

Stone leaned forward, raised a hand and jumped in with, "Well, we're already on the way with the science. As you know, I got the USGS to throw its VDAP team at the problem of just what the tremor means. An array of their new instruments is in place. Now we wait for Mother Earth to cooperate by continuing to shake the ground up there. From my Kilauea experience I'd say we could be lookin' at days, weeks, or even months before we have enough data to pin down the depth where tremor originates. Once we know that, we should be able to track depths to subsequent tremor bursts as they rise toward the surface. An actual eruption will provide the stuff to satisfy those politicians."

He eased back into a very welcoming cushion. There was no surplus WWII furniture in the Chair's office. "Of course, bursts of tremor could stop at any time, leaving us with a dud," Stone added.

"And a thud," Bond added for emphasis. That set Stewart noisily squirming.

"Odds would seem to be in favor of continuing tremors, wouldn't they?" Stewart asked. "They've been coming in off-and-on for a year.

Why would they stop just because of what a few geologists have suddenly decided to do?"

"Whoa!" Stone interjected, staring at Stewart. "What triggers the tremors has nothin' to do with what we humans are up to at the surface. We're nothin' more than incidental jetsam and flotsam on the planet. We're temporary bystanders in the greater scheme of Earth's long history. Nothin' more! N-o-t-h-i-n-g!" Stone slowly spelled out.

Stone paused to let his heated outburst cool a bit. "Meanwhile, though, we can observe and try to understand what's goin' on to the point of makin' meaningful predictions."

Recognizing friction, Bond interrupted. "Okay. Enough, you two. Get moving. Just test and interpret. Test and interpret."

"Later this week we'll be reportin' what we've got to date at the SWGS conference in Tucson," Stone said. "We'll keep watchin' the seismic records as they're beamed to Dick's office in real time, and keep you up to date."

"Okay, guys. Go to it. And, Professor Stone," Bond added, while staring at him, "perhaps wearing something other than a tee-shirt would be a good idea when you speak in Tucson. You *will* be representing NAU."

Stone nodded, gritted his teeth in mock anger, stood, and exited with Stewart close behind.

Friday:

Stone and Stewart had flown to Tucson on Thursday afternoon. The SWGS conference had scheduled their oral presentations back-to-back for Friday morning. Because the topic was a possible near-term volcanic eruption, processing of their abstracts had been expedited. And they would be the lead-off speakers.

About a hundred geologists from five southwestern states assembled for the annual sharing of information. They represented state agencies, the USGS, university professors and students, and some earth-science consulting firms. Other than a few new geology graduate students, attendees knew each other from past years of similar gatherings.

The talks took place in a University of Arizona Geology Department lecture hall. The NAU presentations were especially well attended because the abstracts hinted that a new volcano might be awakening at Toroweap.

Stewart's talk set the stage. He summarized the volcanic history at Toroweap, emphasizing that the Little Springs eruption was only about a thousand years old. He reminded his audience that lava flows of several earlier eruptions at Toroweap had created about twenty lava dams across the Colorado River during the past 800,000 years or so. *I'll bet he had to bite his lip to say those words*, thought Stone. *Or maybe that "or so" phrase at the end covers his biblical butt.* And he described the intermittent tremors that his lone seismometer recorded, as of about a year ago.

The program moderator opened the floor for questions. Predictably, the first was "What do you think the tremors indicate?"

"Excellent question," Stewart responded. "But I'm going to defer an answer, and answers to any other questions related to the tremor, to the next speaker. He'll be able to put tremor into the context of lead-in to actual eruptions. Eruptions at Kilauea in Hawaii."

That was it for Stewart's talk. As he stepped down to join the assembled audience, Stone strode confidently to the podium. His compromise attire, in an attempt to please Chairlady Bond and Stewart, featured an artistic Navajo turquoise bolo tie decorating an open-collar white shirt, tucked into the waistband of new nonprefaded blue Levis. Recently shined black loafers completed what he thought of as a uniform. He was clean-shaven and his hair was combed. His talk began smoothly.

He jumped right into comparing preeruption tremors at Kilauea with those at Toroweap. On a huge screen, he projected representative examples of the seismic wavy tracings of tremor from both places, emphasizing and reemphasizing their virtually identical shapes.

"Study these patterns," Stone said, as he traced them with a laser pointer. "They've got the same wave-lengths, same wave-amplitudes, and same wave-frequencies: about one to two hertz."

He explained that eight newly installed seismometers spread across Toroweap less than a week earlier would now allow the determination of depth to the origin of future tremors and any subsequent decrease of that depth — a sure indicator of impending eruption, based on the Kilauea experience. He seemed to have the audience's rapt attention, waiting anxiously for the next sentence to spill from his lips. That's when his flair for, well, for being himself triggered a silent mental buzz of *what the hell* in his audience as Stone pressed on.

"A separate line of evidence for the magmatic origin of the tremors at Toroweap comes from non-human animal behavior," he said as he clicked his remote image controller. The graph of Jiggles-versus-Rolf filled the screen. This was the first time he had shared this with anyone other than Bonnie.

"Here we see a time-series plot of tremor at Toroweap, as recorded by Doctor Stewart's lone seismometer," Stone said, "versus days when the pet Doberman of the Toroweap park ranger went off his feed in temporary fits of nervousness." An image of a frightened-looking dog decorated the X axis. A wavy line similar to a set of perfectly symmetrical ripples on the surface of a water pond paralleled the Y axis.

Stone pushed on. "There's a clear linear one-to-one relationship between the variables. Dobie Rolf has been too nervous to eat every time tremor shakes the ground at the seismometer. I'm convinced that this correlation reflects a cause-and-effect situation. And that we'll continue to see this relationship as more tremors occur."

Stone paused and could hear, barely, low-volume murmuring.

"Okay," he said. "I know this explanation sounds sort of para-scientific. But my interpretation is based on a similar situation at Kilauea. You all know that I was on the HVO staff there for three years some decades ago. Kilauea erupted several times back then at a location close enough to my little rental house on stilts that the building literally rocked and swayed to the pulsing rhythm of towering lava fountains. My wife Bonnie and I could feel this — barely. We had a pet Doberman at the time. She would whine and tremble until Kilauea quieted down and the tremor stopped."

Don Patchet, the senior seismologist at the University of Arizona, rose and interrupted Stone. "Frank," he said, addressing his remarks to the audience as much as to Stone himself, "we've always appreciated your seat-of-the-pants approach to volcanology down here in our corner of the country. But I think you're now stretching that style to a breaking point."

"Well, Don," Stone responded, "do you have a better explanation for Rolf's behavior?"

The rest of the audience was entertained by this clash between two of their senior respected colleagues. A mini battle of the Titans, right here in a University of Arizona arena.

"Think about this, Frank," Patchet continued. "The tracings of tremor that you've shown us, for both Kilauea and Toroweap, are not part of an actual eruption. At Kilauea they happened during weeks and months preceding eruption. And at this point, we can't even be sure of what is causing the Toroweap tremor. There has been no eruption. Right?"

Stone nodded agreement.

Patchet pushed on. "Also, at Kilauea your dog was *apparently* reacting to shaking caused by a tall surging lava fountain, not some slow hidden subsurface movement of magma that causes ground tremor. For all we know, maybe your pooch could actually *hear* the noise of fountaining and reacted to that, not shaking."

Stone nodded again. "Yes. Fair points, Don," he conceded.

"One more thing, and then I'll sit," Patchet said. "I hope the females in our group won't be offended, but Rolf is male while your Hawaii pet was female. So, could there be a gender difference that needs to be evaluated? Seems to me that your story is poorly thought out — based on a lot of weakly constrained variables."

Patchet's last point stumped Stone. He was so accustomed to living with a female as strong willed as any male he knew, that the notion of a gender factor hadn't occurred to him.

Patchet sat. Stone finished by repeating that the newly installed seismometers would help clarify their working model, once additional bursts of tremor shook the ground.

*　　*　　*

The next morning, the *Tucson Daily's* lead story headlined "NAU Volcanologist Doctor Franklin Stone Predicts Imminent Eruption at Toroweap Based on a Dog's Lack of Appetite."

The following day, Flagstaff's daily paper carried a similar story, though the headline dropped mention of a dog apparently in deference to a nearly native son.

Department Chair Bond was not entertained by the news. She now had an NAU public-relations snafu to clean up. Plus the need to reassure administrators at the other state universities and politicians in Phoenix that Stone was a serious scientist, not a fly-off-the-handle twit. When she called in Stone to confront him about the mess he'd dropped in her lap, he reassured her with "Don't worry. Richard and I are on the right track. Be patient. You'll see." As Stone turned to leave her office, he was sure he noticed her break a smile in reaction to the color photo he handed her, of him standing at the conference podium in his natty attire.

12

THE WAITING GAME

June 1:

Now came the frustrating part of the project — waiting for quaking strong enough to record on the new array of seismometers. When a random person on the street is asked if he or she would like to experience an earthquake, the answer is typically "No!" The mere word earthquake seems to conjure up scenes of death and destruction. However, the VDAP crew, Stone, and Stewart were hoping for a ground shake sooner rather than later. Stone was quite sure that Stewart's hope was in the form of a prayerful request to some higher heavenly being with hands-on control of such things. *Witchcraft!*

Although much distracted by the silence of the seismometers, Stone divorced his mind from Toroweap long enough to finalize his manuscript about the lava dam at Grand Falls. He mailed it to the *Journal of Volcanoes* where it would undergo critiques by two peers. Then he would reply to their comments, and once over that hurdle the paper would be processed by the journal's editorial staff, and reprocessed, and reprocessed, and eventually appear in print.

Stewart seemed to take out his angst of waiting for some new jiggles by extended jogs along the many miles of Flagstaff's forested trails. He had no teaching responsibilities during the summer break of the academic year. He carried a cell phone programmed to vibrate and sing a verse of Onward Christian Soldiers if tremor occurred at Toroweap.

June 6:

Ironically, and perhaps as an omen that something big was in the offing, the first tremor to shake the new system came during the morning of June 6 — D Day for the Toroweap project. Norm Wright of VDAP at Vancouver was in phone contact with Stone and Stewart minutes later.

"Here we go guys," Wright said. "First tremor lasted fifteen minutes. Our automated data-processing system says that it originated about four miles beneath Toroweap. It was recorded by all nine jugs. There's a hint that the seat of tremor is directly beneath a point two miles south of Little Springs cinder cone. For future events, I'll send the results of our data processing electronically."

NAU didn't have the software to process VDAP data.

"No need to phone me with every shake," Wright said. "Just call if you have a question."

"Great!" Stone said. "Thanks Norm," he added. Stone was in his office looking at his geologic map of the Toroweap volcanoes, mentally mapping out possible paths that a new lava flow might follow downslope.

Stewart had interrupted the jog when his phone sang. "And ditto from me, Norm," he shouted. Stewart began sprinting toward his NAU office.

He and Stone huddled to speculate on what the new tremor might mean. Actually, there was little that could be concluded from just one new burst of the jiggles. But at least they now had more reason to feel confident that magma could be slowly rising toward the surface not far south of Little Springs.

Stone phoned Ranger Mark. No answer. He left a message to call if Rolf went off his feed today. The reply came in overnight. "Yes. Rolf refused to eat this morning. He chowed down his evening meal, though." *Another point to add to the Jiggles-versus-Rolf graph. I'll make Don Patchet eat crow, yet.*

Days later:

Starting mid June, events at Toroweap spread in a way that extended the graph's time trend. By the end of June, the seismic network had recorded ten more episodes of tremor. Each originated at shallower depth than its immediate predecessor. Superintendent Clyde Smith of Grand Canyon National Park was kept informed since part of his real estate was at risk of receiving a new coating of lava.

Just before midnight on the Fourth of July, magma appeared at the surface eight miles north of the rim of Grand Canyon and thus became "lava" in the sometimes arcane nomenclature of geology. Same molten-rock stuff, but geologists give it a technical name change when it appears at the surface, free to interact with the atmosphere. *Water to wine. Magma to lava. The molten rock story is not as magical a transition, but sometimes seems as silly,* Stone mused when he was trying to be tolerant of religion's hocus-pocus.

Ranger Mark was awake at his cabin, enjoying a late-night pipe of his favorite smoke, while listening to and singing along with Beatles music. *Lucy in the sky with diamonds. Lucy in the sky with diamonds. Oooooh. Oooooh.*

There were no overnight park visitors to worry about. Rolf suddenly went nearly ballistic. He barked, growled, paced and whined. *What's up friend?* Mark rose slowly from the sofa, nearly floated to the door, and stepped outside. Rolf pushed past him. They were treated to the scene of a towering vertical orange finger of lava on the horizon where the sun had set a few hours earlier. Orange orb down. Orange finger up. *Wow. Far out. What a happy birthday candle for the old USA.*

Mark reassured Rolf that all was okay, went back inside, and tamped another load of fuel into the bowl of his pipe. He decided to phone Stone and Superintendent Smith first thing in the morning. Half an hour later he slowly drifted off to sleep snuggled next to Rolf on the sofa, to the gritty background sound of Bertha rearranging sand in her litter box.

No other humans were near enough to Toroweap to see the spectacle that upset Rolf. Later examination of satellite imagery showed the lava fountain, but Mark was the sole human observer. Unfortunately, for the formal record of eruption, Mark had been a bit too relaxed to think of capturing a digital image or two of the thousand-foot-tall blade of molten basalt pointing toward the moon.

13

GOING WITH THE FLOW

The onset of eruption triggered an alert at CVO, which triggered a call to Wright at home in Vancouver. Something had gone awry with the seismic array. A sleepy sounding Wright phoned Stone and Stewart, who listened to him explain that what the seismometers were now recording was almost certainly an eruption. Stone went to the kitchen to avoid waking Bonnie. He heard the crying of young kids in the background at the Stewart end of their connection.

"The shaking is steady and way more violent than normal tremor," Wright said. "We've lost signals from two of the instruments closest to the surface target that rising magma seems to have aimed for. Those jugs have likely been buried by lava. I've been through this before. I advise you guys to get up there ASAP for some ground truth!"

"Understood," said Stone. "Thanks Norm. You deserve a gold star on your report card for keepin' such late hours."

"Don't give a damn about a star of any color," Wright said. "But I wouldn't mind a bump in my salary. Being on twenty-four-hour VDAP call can get old fast."

Stone thought Norm didn't sound nearly as grumpy as his words suggested.

"Gotta admit, though," Wright continued, "the travel perks are great. I've already seen more of the world than most folks, including the rich, ever will. Seen some incredible eruptions, too, without getting burned. And I'm still twenty years from retirement."

"I can identify with ya there," Stone said. "Now, get some sleep. We'll take care of the situation and get back to you sometime after the sun peeks up."

"Ditto what Franklin said," added Stewart.

Stone and Stewart stayed on the line after Norm signed off. "What do we do, now, boss?" Stewart asked.

"Here's what I suggest," Stone replied. "I'll drive up in my 4x4 pickup right now. Once the sun peeks up, you grab an NAU van and supplies to cover food, drinks and what not for a few days. Then hit the road as soon as possible. Take time to get your family settled in, though, in case we stay very long."

"Okay," Stewart said. "And Franklin," he added after a slight pause, "thanks for thinking of my family. That's real Christ — uh, very thoughtful of you."

"Don't give it a second thought," Stone hastily added. "Some of the nicest people I know are atheists — or agnostics."

He hesitated briefly, realizing he'd just been a bit unnecessarily nasty.

"Some are Christians, too," Stone said.

However much he distanced himself from organized religion of all ilks, Stone recognized people like Stewart as kind folks who treated fellow humans, humanely.

Stone woke Bonnie to explain what was happening. He would stay in touch by phone. He then punched in Mark's number. No answer. He donned his lava-chasing attire and hit the road. Traffic was so light at night that he managed to greatly exceed the legal speed limit, without encountering a red-light-and-siren police car. Another bit of reckless behavior was a phone call at 80 miles per hour to leave a message of "probable eruption underway at Toroweap" on Superintendent Clyde Smith's answering service.

Stone arrived at Toroweap shortly after sunrise. It was another cloud-free spring day in northern Arizona. About the only daily weather variable this time of year was wind velocity. Today's blow was a light breeze.

He decided to check on Mark and his menagerie first. As he drove up to the house, Mark was outside throwing a ball for Rolf. Rolf ignored the ball long enough to do the doggie crotch sniff, when Stone slid out of his truck.

"Hey Mark. How goes it?" Stone asked.

"Hi, Frank," Mark replied, in his usual slow-and-low, drawn-out voice. "Didn't expect to see you here this time of day. I was about to call you and my boss — soon as Rolf gets his morning exercise. 'Cause hey, either I was hallucinating last night, or an eruption started over towards Little Springs." He rubbed tired-looking eyes and pointed to the northwest.

"I wouldn't be a bit surprised if you were in a hallucinatin' mood last night," Stone said. "But, yeah, you probably did see the start of an eruption. I got a midnight call from the VDAP folks. The earthquake jugs were shakin' like hell. Two of 'em stopped broadcastin' info. Probably destroyed by lava."

"Cool," Mark drawled. "I've never been to an eruption before. Look over there." He pointed toward Little Springs. A faint plume of smoke was rising, rooted off in the direction where Mark said he saw action last night.

"That smoke's probably comin' from a small fire started by lava," Stone said. "I'm drivin' up by Little Springs right now. You should call your boss and tell him what's up. You're safe here. This ain't a Mount St. Helens. Keep your phone on."

Stone's phone then buzzed. It was a call from Stewart. He was loading gear into an NAU truck and would be on the road within an hour.

"I'll be up near where we camped at the edge of the Little Springs flow," Stone told him. "Meet me there."

"Will do," Stewart replied. "And Franklin, I've briefed Bond on what's happening."

"Well done," said Stone.

From that campsite, the smoke plume was south and a little east. Stone filled his pack with water and snacks and hiked off in that direction, after leaving a note for Stewart, pinned under a windshield wiper.

An hour later he was within a Stone's throw from where orange/red molten basalt oozed onto the surface and flowed downhill, in a dry stream channel. He pulled a handheld recorder from his pack and started talking into it.

It's eight AM on July fifth. I'm at the vent for the Toroweap eruption that began last night around midnight. Basalt is oozing quietly and steadily out and feedin' a narrow channelized flow headed south to southeast. Can't see the downstream snout from here. Flow's about twenty feet thick, sixty feet wide and moving at the speed of a brisk walk. It's as though a giant asbestos garden hose is feedin' molten basalt into a riverbed. Ranger Mark says he saw a tall fountain of lava from his quarters last night. That must not have lasted long, 'cause there's only about fifty feet of agglutinated spatter built up like a collar around the vent. The rising magma must have been volatile poor, or it would have produced a lot more spatter. It's a case of the barely carbonated soda pop syndrome. I'm takin' a rock sample near the vent. Then I'm headed back to my truck to drive down to Ranger Mark's place. I'm pretty sure the lava flow is headed in that direction. Really nothin' else I can do here now.

Back at the truck, he tore up the note to Stewart, phoned him and told him to meet at Mark's house.

Stewart pulled in during early afternoon. Stone was there waiting, standing in the shade of the equipment shed, talking on his cell to update Bonnie. Mark was inside his house, feeding Finny and Bertha. Stewart parked and jumped out, looking pretty stoked. And that stoked Stone.

"Okay, Dick," Stone said. "You're in for a treat. First time of encountering live lava. I'll never forget my first. Read all the text books you want, but there's nothin' like seein', hearin', breathin', and feelin' the stuff that comes from molten basalt right there at your feet. And then, after you've watched for awhile, you can dip your geology pick into that oozin' taffy-like goo and collect a sample that's as untainted as it gets."

Stone was feeling a bit mystical, talking to himself more than the person facing him. His memory of his first time with live lava took him back to Kilauea. He hadn't described it this way to Bonnie, but that first was about as memorable as losing his virginity with her.

"Franklin," Stewart cried. "Franklin! Are you with me?"

"Yeah, sure," Stone sighed. "Pack up what you'll want for the next few hours. We're gonna hike uphill in the Little Springs direction to find the front of the lava flow."

He walked to the house to tell Mark what he and Stewart were up to. "And keep your cell phone on. It's important that we can stay in touch." Mark mumbled something about Smith as Stone walked away.

Stone and Stewart drove a mile or so to the base of where the landscape steepened toward Little Springs. That was the far western side of the park's landing strip for small aircraft. As they were about to start walking, the thwap thwap sound of whirling helicopter blades to the south broke the silence. They watched as the four-passenger machine approached and landed near their truck.

As rotating blades slowed and quieted, a man that Stone recognized emerged from the passenger side and joined them. He changed from crash helmet to wide-brimmed Smokey-the-Bear hat in the process. His official green park service shirt was decorated with the shiny brass words *Clyde Smith, Superintendent*. Color-coordinated pants were neatly pressed. Shoes were polished. He was clean shaven. The only apparent mar to his persona was a small red spot on his lightly tanned cheek, apparently where a razor blade had cut below whisker level. He looked so fastidiously neat and newly polished, that a squeak might be expected when he moved. This was a man whose job was to deal with and impress the millions of visitors who came to see his national park each year.

Stone knew him from earlier business related to the geology of the park. A quick handshake, then Smith said, "Frank, thanks for your call. Seems my Ranger Mark up here thinks I don't need to know about an erupting volcano in my park. He did call, though. About ten minutes ago as we flew over the Hualapai Indian Reservation. I've got a love/hate relationship with that guy. He gets consistently good reports from his visitors. But he seems to think that Toroweap is his personal domain, rather than part of the public's Grand Canyon National Park. He's lasted longer than most up here though, and that's a real plus for me."

Stone nodded in understanding of the situation, and said, "He's been very cooperative with us. I think he's an okay guy. Just pretty laid back. He knows what needs doin' but he's not in a hurry to get it done. I see some of a younger me in him."

Smith smiled, remembering the hallway and party-time tales about Stone's antics during his years at HVO.

"So what's happening?" Smith asked. "My pilot and I saw a bit of smoke from a couple of burning trees up near Little Springs. We're cursed with too many of those now with the drought we're in. But we didn't see any evidence of eruption."

"Well there's an eruption, alright," Stone replied. "So now you get to worry about a volcano setting fires, in addition to careless campers and lightning. I was up by Little Springs this morning and found where molten stuff is oozing out of the ground — a little south of Little Springs. Dick and

I were just startin' to walk towards where I saw that. We'll get an idea of how fast the lava is flowin' toward the canyon. We'll be able to figure out the route it'll take movin' in that direction, too, I think. There's enough hilly relief to keep the flow channeled, instead of just spreadin' out."

Stone paused briefly to think beyond the science.

"Meanwhile," he added. "I think you should spread word of the eruption to rafters that have permits to float through the canyon. Dick and I will keep you updated on what we find."

"Yes, do," said Smith. "I need to be kept in the loop. And I'm not sure I can depend on Mark."

"I understand," said Stone. "Will do."

"Good," Smith said. "Thanks guys. And be careful."

As Stone and Stewart headed into the hilly country towards Little Springs, the chopper went airborne, circled over the source of smoke, and then turned southeast toward the South Rim and Park Headquarters.

Back in Flagstaff, Chairlady Crystal Bond was working the university and the politicians in Phoenix, telling them of the ongoing eruption at Toroweap. An eruption that had been foreseen and essentially predicted by professors Franklin Stone and Richard Stewart of her department. The on-campus NPR affiliate KNAU was broadcasting news of the eruption hourly.

Stone and Stewart were soon standing beside the leading snout of a lava river. In his excitement of a memorable first, Stewart forgot his promise to Stone and repeatedly thanked a mythical being upstairs for providing such an incredible event that would save his job and family security.

Stone let him pontificate. First lava was a surreal experience whatever one's views of religion might be. So he wouldn't spoil Stewart's joy by pointing out that a volcanic eruption is Earth's way of quickly expelling part of its vast and continually renewing internal storehouse of heat. Eruptions had to happen, from time to time, unless all the discoveries of science were malarkey. And they would continue to happen, until the heat-producing radioactive chemical elements in Earth decayed away. Given the Earth's history of 4.5 billion years of radioactive heat generation to date, combined with some half-lives in the billions of years, that wouldn't happen soon. Meanwhile, a useful pursuit for curious humans was to try to predict exactly when and where eruptions would take place. For the incurious, well . . .

"Frank to Richard," Stone eventually said. "Frank to Richard. Time to rejoin Earth. By the way. When are you gonna get some real hikin' boots to replace those silly Nikes?"

Stewart ignored that comment, rebooted his mind, and said. "What now?"

"Let's head back to the truck," Stone proposed. "We can shortcut and get there before the lava does."

And they did. They moved the truck to the east side of the landing strip and watched as the slowly advancing toe of the lava river rounded a final bend in the hilly landscape and began to spread laterally and pond in the broad, nearly flat-floored basin of the Toroweap airport.

14

LIVE-LAVA BED

The rest of July, plus August:

Flow of lava onto the airfield was eerily quiet and remained non-life threatening. Except for the immediate vicinity of the vent and the very distal front of the advancing flow, fiery-red molten basalt was not visible. Between those endpoints a solid rocky crust of hot black basalt enveloped and insulated a liquid core. It was quenched by contact with an atmosphere whose temperature is about two thousand degrees lower than the freezing point of liquid basalt.

Had an uninformed, daydreaming stranger happened to walk a path that crossed this hidden river of lava, that person might have discovered what was underfoot only when shoe soles began to smoke and melt. A non-daydreamer would have felt the heat in time to avoid setting foot on an obviously new lava surface.

Within several days, a crusted-over pad of lava covered the entire airport basin. Continuing inflow from the vent through the lava tube then began inflating this gigantic pancake-shaped bladder as it lifted and spread laterally against and up surrounding gentle slopes.

Ranger Mark's home was safely higher than even a filled-to-overflowing airfield would be. Park campgrounds were to remain open so long as Stone's daily evaluation of the situation was *safe*. Rolf's bouts with tremor-induced fear were gone. Bertha and Finney had no idea that an eruption was underway. Park visitation for Toroweap was setting new records. Advanced overnight reservations were required as campground capacities were otherwise regularly exceeded. Most visitors were displeased that a maximum stay of three consecutive days was strictly enforced. The increase in Ranger Mark's maintenance chores increased his need for stress-reducing evening pipe smokes. Smokes came after his daily phone call to update Superintendent Smith.

At Flagstaff, Crystal Bond found the university and political systems lubricated for NAU to a degree never before seen. Her department's seismicity program would be preserved and expanded by one tenure-track faculty position. Additional funding that came with this growth was everything Bond had requested.

The formerly quiet, reserved, and hermit-like Professor Richard Stewart walked the academic halls exuding an aura of confidence and accomplishment. With his share of the scientific discoveries related to the ongoing eruption came a salary bump. Said bump, combined with new job security, was soon followed by his announcement that wife Sarah was pregnant and growing a bump containing the formative child number eight.

Stone's NAU salary remained at zero. But the Geology Department paid rent for a travel trailer. Stone parked it near Ranger Mark's house and tapped into NPS propane, electricity, and water. He was there to track the eruption and advise if the situation became threatening to park visitors or property. Bonnie locked their Flagstaff house and moved to Toroweap. She became a stringer, reporting for the Flagstaff daily newspaper. Her first story ran above the fold of page one. Stone's plot of Jiggles-versus-Rolf was the featured graphic. Stone sent a copy to Professor Patchet in Tucson.

Wright and crew visited from CVO Vancouver long enough to retrieve the seismometers that had not been buried by lava. The new instruments had proven themselves ready for foreign deployment.

Stone was inundated by geologists visiting from Arizona's universities and from neighboring states. None had ever before seen a volcanic eruption underway, and this one was so safely approachable. Lessons learned were of the ilk impossible to reproduce in a sit-down classroom setting. Stone gained new friends, professional colleagues, and fame.

Yet, in spite of such excitement, by the end of July the daily routine was weighing on Stone. A new variety of ennui was creeping into his psyche. His bucket list had indeed been updated with the eruption, but he now wanted short-term closure of this project — short-term relative to his remaining years, however many they might prove to be. *Keep it movin'. Keep it movin',* was a recurring thought.

He proposed naming the new volcano JR, to recognize the contributions of jiggles and Rolf. With some help from Bonnie's stream of published essays, that name stuck.

Bonnie was ecstatic with her daily task of cranking out another update for the newspaper. She made comparisons to other volcanoes, and speculated in ways that no scientist could do. The public loved her arm waving. She had a damn good start of what might become a novel. At the end of each day, just before going to bed, she added another page to her life-with-Frank diary.

Meanwhile, for Stone, no signs that eruption was slowing or accelerating translated into frustration. Same old, same old, day after day. This routine was becoming boringly routine. Once a week, he visited the vent where he saw the same sight — magma magically becoming lava by geologic command, and feeding into an insulated tube that carried that hot stuff to the airfield.

There, each day, he walked the perimeter of the slowly growing lava bladder. By measuring the uptick in vertical angle from a series of positions around the inflating system, he could estimate the slow rise of the top. Primitive, but effective. No high-tech needed. He also measured the horizontal distance from his perimeter sites to the slowly expanding outer edge of the bladder. To feel useful, he spent parts of evenings plotting the changes of his measurements versus time. Two new X-versus-Y graphs, with no doubt about cause and effect. Night after night, after a couple of Cuba libre's his mind would drift to *Keep blowin' air into a balloon and it gets bigger. Big effin' deal.*

Finally, late August brought welcome change. The top of the live-lava bed became stagnant. No more uplift. Simultaneously, the entire perimeter, save one sector along the south edge, stopped moving outward and upward. That sector continued to move out, southward, but now at several times the velocity of previous weeks. The lowest point on the rim surrounding the airport basin had been surmounted. *Too much air into a balloon and it's gonna pop. Too much lava added to my container means it's gonna overflow. Yes! Yes! It's headin' south, right toward Vulcan's Throne. It's*

2

2

time to talk turkey with Clyde. Maybe we can slow the flow long enough to avoid creatin' a new lava dam in the Grand Canyon. Or maybe he's got other priorities.

He requested a meeting at Toroweap with Superintendent Smith, and Chairlady Bond. Stewart and Tony Piedras, a representative from the Arizona Geological Survey, invited themselves. Bonnie would gather info for news stories, while serving the group drinks and snacks.

15

MAN VERSUS VOLCANO

Late August, early afternoon:

Now well into Arizona's rainy monsoon season, the assembled group met inside Ranger Mark's house to escape a downpour that had begun, following a morning cloud buildup. Climate change had greatly reduced annual rainfall in the Southwest. But the occasional monsoon soaker still rolled in between July and September. And when it rained, it *rained*. Hard. At the moment, a thin disc of steam rose steadily from the hot, bloated lava bladder that covered the former airfield. A bit higher, golden eagles, red-tailed hawks, and California condors soared overhead, searching for lunch. One could only guess how many burrowing rodents were now trapped underground, beneath the lava bladder. Most would have a hellishly long horizontal dig to escape its footprint. Condors would clean up any leftovers. The overall scene mimicked that of a low-budget Hollywood sci-fi flick. But this was for real.

Overnight stays by visitors were no longer allowed in the Toroweap section of the park. Superintendent Smith, quite reasonably, had decided that the two campsites were potential targets of the advancing lava. Even if the campsites themselves weren't buried by new basalt, the dead-end access road to them was already within reach of the hot stuff. Outside park boundaries, a steady stream of adventurous gawkers continued to hike to the erupting vent and along its downstream hot-roofed lava tube. Stone guesstimated that these visitors had already carted away at least a ton of souvenir chunks of the new lava. *For bragging rights only? The stuff looks just like its Little Springs neighbor.*

Back at camp, Bonnie had tidied up Ranger Mark's messy quarters before visitors arrived. She opened windows and the door, which helped freshen inside air. She prepared a large urn of coffee for the group, and the night before had whipped up a batch of brownies for snacks. Cups, sugar, cream, and napkins sat next to the urn. Cans of fruit juice sat beside a No Caffeine sign. Stone brought folding camp chairs from the travel trailer so all could sit. They numbered seven.

Bertha was "quarantined" in a cardboard pet box for the duration. If put outside, she would likely become raptor food. Rolf rested quietly in the sleeping-quarters end of the building, once he completed his rounds of crotch sniffing for all new humans present.

Stone would lead the discussion. Though Stewart was a co-discovery scientist for the now-active volcanic eruption, he was content with being a silent observer in the background. His earlier role had gained him job security, and a salary raise. Further recognition and praise for his part in advancing science was a distant second place on his priority list.

The group shared hellos and handshakes all around. While others sat, Stone stood near the entry door, facing the sofa and chairs. He painted his face with what he hoped was a serious-looking expression and began.

"Welcome to Toroweap, home of the one and only ongoing volcanic eruption in the lower forty-eight. I think you all know the general status of that action. In particular, the airfield is filled to overflowing now, and a tongue of lava is creepin' toward the canyon. It's got a few miles to go. At the present rate, it'll take weeks. But we should develop a plan now — a plan for what, if anything, we might do to change the speed and direction of the flow."

Superintendent Smith reached out his right arm, with fist clenched and thumb up. "Totally agree," he said. "I've got a responsibility for the safety of all park visitors, including groups rafting down the river."

Stone continued, "Right. So, first of all, I want to be crystal clear about one thing." He hesitated a few seconds for emphasis. "Nothing, and I mean *absolutely* nothing we might do in reaction to the lava flow and its march toward the canyon can control what nature is up to. Redirect and maybe even temporarily slow the flow? Maybe. But control the eruption? No way."

Gesticulating arms and animated hands added emphasis. He paused to slurp coffee, spilling some on a tee-shirt whose message was "Volcanoes are Hotties."

He continued, "Yes. Our fancy seismic jugs were able to more-or-less foresee the where and when of an impending eruption. Thank you VDAP folks." He saluted in the general direction of Vancouver, Washington.

He then paused, smiled, and changed his voice to a low-volume mock-secretive whisper. "Incidentally, I thank Rolf for contributing to that success."

That brought a chuckle from the group. The good-natured open debate between Stone and Don Patchet about the possible role of animal behavior in sensing earth tremors had become popular with the reading public. Bonnie had helped grease the skids of that topic with her daily newspaper stories. In earthquake- and volcano-prone regions, Doberman Breeders of America was reporting a surge in requests for referrals to Doberman breeders. Hearing his name, alert Rolf peeked around the half-wall of the sleeping area and yipped. "That's my man, Rolf. Stay alert," Stone said. Rolf retreated into his snooze posture. Stone reverted to his serious-sounding tone.

"The good news is that the kind of eruption we've got at Toroweap isn't one of those so-called Super Volcano blasts," Stone said. "You know, the kind that the BBC sensationalized on TV some years back. We don't have to worry about another Yellowstone here. Or even a Mount St. Helens. We're dealin' with what's called a basalt cinder cone eruption. Think of Sunset Crater. Think of a baby in the greater volcano family. There's lots and lots of them. But no one of 'em is very big and destructive. JR is another of the Little Springs variety. But a version that keeps oozing lava for a longer time than Little Springs did."

Stone paused for another sip of coffee, to give his listeners time to digest what they just heard. Smith grabbed a brownie, bit off a chunk, and noisily chewed. He was a bachelor, who was widely known as someone who couldn't cook. The many hosted social events that came with his position were all professionally catered.

"The thing is," Stone continued, "geologists are gettin' better and better in predicting when and where an eruption like this will take place. But they don't know diddly-squat about predicting when it'll *stop* once it's underway. Historic examples like the one goin' on here lasted a few days. Others went on for several years, even for a decade or more. Not to sound too hopeless, but once an eruption gets underway, humans just have to go with the flow. There's no magic cork to shove down the neck of an erupting vent."

Stone was sounding and acting as adult as he could muster. Those who knew him well would have been impressed — maybe even a bit surprised. Of the present group, only Bonnie and perhaps Chairlady Bond were of that ilk. The others would assume that indeed he was drop-dead serious. And he was, in his own informal, earthy way.

"Okay," Stone said. "So here's what we can consider usin' as tools." He paused briefly and inhaled deeply. "Bombs, water, D-10 Cats," he said, lifting an additional finger of his right hand with each item.

Recitation of that list triggered laughter, followed by *what the hell* expressions, and head scratching.

"Get serious, Stone," Smith said. "I didn't come all the way up here to listen to a fantasy tale. The only item on that list that I would welcome into the park is water. We can always use more potable water up here. D-10s and bombs are for destroying a natural landscape, not rescuing and preserving it."

"Understood," Stone replied. "But listen up before you close and lock the doors of your park."

He focused on Smith and continued. "Sprayin' water on a flow cools and speeds up the solidification of the lava. It kinda builds an instantly thick solid rind to keep still-liquid stuff trapped. This saved lots of buildings at Heimaey in Iceland some years back. I can direct you to literature about that, if you want the details."

Smith nodded.

Stone continued. "Pushed-up berms as dams have also created extra rescue time at places like Etna and Hawaii. That's where the D-10s, or their Italian equivalents, come in. There are published reports about that stuff, too. This ain't science fiction folks."

No, it wasn't science fiction, but it was a lot for non-volcano people to quickly digest. So Stone paused again, to sip coffee.

He then continued with his primer on man-versus-volcano. "Back around the mid nineteen hundreds, aerial bombing was tried a couple times in Hawaii. The idea was to change the path of lava comin' from Mauna Loa, so Hilo wouldn't be overrun. That didn't really get tested, 'cause the eruption stopped way short of the town. I think that bombing was mostly an excuse for the U.S. Army Air Corps flyboys to have some fun practice, anyway. I'll gladly take that tool off my list of useful eruption controls."

"It would *never* be on *my* list," Smith said.

That comment triggered a reflex in Stone's psyche. There was another volcano-control tool used by some — a tool that would *never be* on Stone's list. He hadn't planned on talking about it, but Smith unknowingly opened a door that Stone now strode through.

"One last anecdote, just for the record," he began. "Primitive, faith-based folks have offered virgins and other gifts to volcano deities in attempts to stop unwanted destruction. Hawaiians today frequently offer gifts to the mythical Pele. They throw money, flowers, food, and booze into Halemaumau and other craters, hoping that Pele will be pleased enough to avoid harming the people who live on her Big-Island home."

Stone paused, then said, "But don't get me started on describing details of all the times Pele did not seem to be pleased or placated by the gifts. Since humans arrived to inhabit her islands, more homes have been burned, and people maimed or killed than we have time to review here. We should simply believe in my coffee cup message." He flashed the cup's Volcanoes Rule side to the group.

Stone decided to go on with one more example of the deity sort. "In the early nineteen forties in Mexico, an eruption like the one goin' on here began in a farmer's corn field. During the next nine years, lava oozed miles northward, destroying all buildings and cornfields in its path. Local folks tried to stop this with marches and prayers. Their reward, if you want to call it that, was that their church steeple avoided complete burial. It still sticks up like an unfinished demolition project today."

He paused to clear his throat. Then he summed up with, "Prayers, deities, and such are less effective than water and D-10s."

By now, Stewart was frowning. Stone wasn't sure about the religious leanings of the rest of his audience. But he'd made his point, and moved right along to avoid possible awkward debate related to supernatural stuff.

"So." Stone looked directly at Smith. "Maybe we can use water and D-10s? I think our main concern is to somehow keep lava from spillin' into the canyon. Otherwise, we're lookin' at an unwanted dam, and all the complications up- and down-stream that would come with it. Another episode like one of those twenty or so lava dams that came, created a lake, and eventually burst — not all that long before humans arrived on the scene here."

Nods of agreement and softly voiced *yeahs*, cemented that point.

Stone, encouraged, said, "My idea is to keep the lava from reachin' the canyon rim for as long as possible. And hope — really *hope* that meanwhile, JR runs out of magma. That happened naturally with Little Springs. Maybe that can happen now, with some intervention by us."

Stone sipped coffee again. Others followed suit, as Stewart slurped Crapple juice. The last brownies disappeared.

Superintendent Smith spoke next. "Do you have an estimate of the odds of the eruption stopping if we can dam the front of the flow, say for a few weeks or so?"

"None," Stone said. "I don't even want to go on record with a so-called ballpark guesstimate. But at least we can buy some time, and maybe even win the game. It's possible. But probable? I don't know. No sense trying to paint a rosy picture without a useful brush.

"Dick?" Stone asked, looking at Stewart. "Any thoughts?" Stewart shook his head no.

"Tony?"

"I've never before seen a live eruption or read much about them," Piedras said. "I won't even try to make a stab at what to do about the eruption. I'm mostly here to gather information about statewide interests."

Stone looked toward the final person who might have scientific input to offer. "Chairlady Bond?" he asked.

"With regard to the science part, I'll go along with whatever you recommend, Franklin," she said, in thoughtful measured cadence. "You've been the key to the best understanding of this situation all along. You're the only one of us who has ever dealt with actual eruptions."

"But with regard to institutional legal interests," she added after a noticeable pause. She focused her attention on Superintendent Smith, "I believe that NAU will need a clear statement that the National Park Service approves of whatever actions are agreed to by us here today with regard to influencing the advance and path of the lava flow."

"Yes. I understand that concern," Smith replied. "Once I get my marching orders from Washington, I'll send you a letter of legal agreement between the Park Service and NAU."

"Fine," Bond said.

The ensuing silence, as they say, spoke volumes. Through all of this, glazed-eyed Ranger Mark looked as though he had just enjoyed a pipe or two of his favorite smoke. Bonnie kept silent while scribbling notes for her next article. Stone rubbed his neck and then his tiring left knee. He was ready to sit.

Superintendent Smith then said, "I agree that we should try to keep lava from spilling into the canyon, but . . ." He shook his head from side to side. "I'll have to get permission from the Secretary of the Interior to mess with nature in the park. Maybe he'll go for something that might keep lava out of the canyon. I just don't know."

"Okay, I understand the politics of that," Stone said. "But ask him today! We need to move if we expect to slow or divert the flow at all."

Stone grinned and added, "I'll bet Mark's water supply is pretty low. How about you order two or three large tanker trucks to get out here tomorrow? They should come with powerful pumps and long hoses, for sprayin'." Superintendent Smith nodded agreement.

With that suggestion, the meeting was over. Smith told Mark to order water. The hour was too late to contact his Washington D.C. superiors. He promised Stone that he would make that call first thing the following day and pressure the secretary for permission to spray water on the lava. If the answer was no, Ranger Mark would have water to last a long time for his household use.

Smith also promised Stone that he would seek permission for pushing up a flow-stopping berm with D-10 Cats. Then Bond, Stewart, and Piedras began the drive back to Flagstaff, while Smith headed to his South Rim park office.

*   *   *

Early the next morning, Smith phoned Stone to say that the water treatment was a go. By mid-afternoon, three ten-thousand-gallon water tankers arrived. In sequence, each driver sprayed his load across the leading edge of the lava. Dense white condensation clouds from the vaporized liquid obscured what was happening to the lava. Two hours later, the air cleared and Stone reoccupied his surveying stations. The snout of the lava had moved down slope only a few feet during the past twenty-four hours, a mere trickle compared to the average rate of advance before the water dousing. Ranger Mark ordered three more truckloads of water for the next day.

The water treatment continued into a third day. Ninety thousand gallons of water temporarily increased the relative humidity at Toroweap. But Stone's daily surveying measurements showed that even though the lava advance had slowed by the cooling, it surged some hours after water treatment ceased. It was as though water chill modified what had been a smooth and continuous downstream waltz into a jerky two-step advance. Meanwhile, the rate of eruption at the JR vent was steady. From there, new lava moved down the tube, into the airfield bladder, and out the downslope side toward Vulcan's Throne. Stone was playing a losing game. He told Mark to terminate water deliveries, and phoned Superintendent Smith.

"Hi Clyde," Stone began. "It's Frank Stone up here at Toroweap. The water treatment isn't doin' the trick. It temporarily slows the lava advance. But by the time the next round of water truckloads arrives the flow is back to normal speed. Makes no sense to continue this dance."

"But you said this worked in Iceland," Smith said, sounding a bit exasperated. "What's different here? Water is water. Right?"

Stone hesitated, knowing that all along he had considered the water ploy at Toroweap unlikely to work. A possible ploy, but not very probable. But, damn, he liked to tinker with volcanoes. *Buddies and I even tried to trigger an eruption by dumping explosives into a huge roiling lake of molten basalt in a crater at Kilauea. We hoped to make it boil over. We failed. But the experiment sure was fun!*

"Well," Stone began to explain, "I guess water worked in Iceland 'cause the lava flow was near the seacoast. They had all the water in the Atlantic Ocean as their delivery tankers. All they had to do was throw a hose into the briny and start pumpin' and sprayin'. We can't come close to reproducin' that kind of situation here. We'd need every damn tanker truck in the region runnin' nonstop. And given our recent drier climate, water supply is limited even if we had the trucks. We might suck Lake Powell completely dry in the process."

He let that info sink into Smith's mind for a few moments and then added, "What do you think about the D-10 plan?"

"Believe it or not," Smith said, "D.C. says it's a go. They really really don't want lava spilling into the canyon. And they figure that if a pushed-up berm stops that from happening, it could even become a historic teaching tool in the park."

Smith paused to clear his throat, and then said, "Interesting, isn't it, how justification for defacing a national park landscape can be rationalized with a simplistic *aha* teaching tool." The tone of his voice reeked with disapproval.

Stone kept his childish enthusiasm for the D-10 tactic silently in check. Then he said, "If it helps soothe your feelings about what's happenin' to your park, I really do think the odds of the D-10 berm stopping the lava flow are better than the water cooling treatment."

"Thanks, Frank," Smith said. "I appreciate that thought. So, go ahead and get the D-10s working."

*   *   *

Stone had anticipated the go-ahead, with phone calls that located a couple of currently idle Cats in Page, Arizona. By noon the next day, two of the big powerful dirt pushers were loudly belching exhaust into the still air of Toroweap. A thousand-gallon tanker truck of diesel fuel came with them.

Ranger Mark and Rolf were fascinated with the noisy goings-on. Park visitors were not allowed in the area, so Mark had no campsite duties. He set up a shaded chair and a bowl of water for Rolf, and watched the Cats as he pleasantly puffed on his favorite pipe tobacco.

The Cats worked a mile in front of the slowly advancing lava, pushing whatever their blades could dislodge into the flow's drainage path. They alternated between adding to the pile and crisscrossing it, blade up, to help pack the debris into something more substantial than loose sand, gravel, and larger chunks of rock.

Within a week they had created a forty-foot-tall substantial obstruction across the dry ravine whose upstream bed was being incrementally filled with two-thousand-degree lava delivered by the JR pipeline. Stone phoned a report to Smith, and attached photos to an e-mail. Bonnie sent another essay to the Flagstaff daily. The bottom line for both missives was: *Now we wait and watch.*

September arrived. NAU was back in session. The college football team continued its lackluster losing tradition. Aspen leaves turned to their almost magical quaking performances of yellowish gold. Elk hunters bagged meat that would last through winter — tough to chew, but hormone free. A few campfires somehow grew into forest conflagrations of dead or nearly dead ponderosa pines, weakened by the persistent drought of global climate change, superposed on longer-term bark-beetle infestations. Flagstaff city planners announced they would continue to devote so-called waste water to the creation of artificial snow, to the commercial benefit of the area's one downhill ski resort. Life went on, as though climate change and a nearby erupting volcano didn't matter.

Bonnie moved back to town. Stone stayed at Toroweap to monitor the advance of lava toward the D-10 berm. He was determined to see the last adventure of his bucket list to completion. He vowed to not kick that empty container until the JR eruption stopped. He had high hopes for what that end result would be. Kilauea eruptions had been exciting events in his professional life. But the thought of seeing liquid basalt spilling thousands of feet into the Grand Canyon to create a dam and water reservoir would be the best frosting he could imagine on a real retirement cake. Nature said that the heat engine in planet Earth was in charge of when and what the result of the JR eruption would be.

The snout of lava was now a bit less than a mile from the berm. Stone measured the advance daily, and calculated that basalt would meet berm around mid October. Meanwhile he spent considerable time with Ranger Mark and the pets. Eventually, a second pipe appeared from the ranger's cupboard. The two puffed and reminisced, Stone about his Hawaiian years where *pakalōlō* flourished, and Ranger Mark about his pre-park-service years hanging with U.C. Santa Barbara students in Isla Vista, California. Their shared time passed peacefully, pleasantly, and often gigglingly.

October 17, mid afternoon:

"Happy Birthday, Bonnie," Stone chirped at his end of their phone connection. "What's the plan for your special day?"

She'd been expecting a birthday call. October 17 was one of two dates that Stone would never forget. The other was their December 5th wedding anniversary. Stone had learned to not forget these days, during their very first year of marriage. Bonnie was traditional about such stuff.

"Not much, my man," Bonnie said. "I'll be dining with some of my writer friends at the Weatherford Hotel tonight. Catered meal. We're renting a private room upstairs so we can be crazy if we choose to."

Silence, then, "You still there Frank?" Bonnie asked.

"Sure," Stone whispered. "God, I miss you. So much." He sounded teary.

"Hey, no need for such blather," Bonnie chastened her husband. "Whenever you slip up and use that particular three-letter G word, I know you're in a bad spot. I miss you too, lover."

"Hangin' with Mark and his menagerie has some perks that help the time go," Stone explained. "But it's really really *hard* bein' up here so long without you."

"Yeah, I understand," Bonnie said. "Just make sure you're still bein' that way when we get back together. We'll make up for lost time."

Seriousness instantly morphed into laughter.

"Enough entertainment for the NSA," Stone said. "Now, here's your very special and unique birthday present. Ready?"

"Oh yeah!" Bonnie chimed.

"Exactly one hour ago," Stone began slowly to help build suspense, "lava kissed berm."

"Finally!" Bonnie shouted jubilantly. Stone pulled his phone away from a ringing eardrum.

"Yup!" Stone said. "And I watched it happen."

"So now what?" Bonnie asked.

"We wait," the scientist side of Stone proclaimed. "If JR keeps sending new stuff down the tube, that berm doesn't have a chance in hell of stoppin' the flow. It'll hold for awhile, but eventually it'll get overrun and bulldozed away. All I can do is watch and wait. I'd never say so to Clyde, but I've got my fingers crossed to see a new lava dam in the canyon. His job could get real complicated if that happens. But the finale of my bucket list would be incredible. I might even really retire, then."

Silence reflected daydreaming at both ends of the conversation.

"Keep me posted, lover," Bonnie finally said. "I'll be staying up late after tonight's dinner party. Got a hot new story to write for the daily, don't I!"

Following faux kisses, they said goodbye.

16

BYE BYE BERM: HELLO CANYON

November:

It took two weeks of lava build-up and push for the berm to fail. During that wait, Stone liked to walk across the top of the berm and taunt the lava with shouts of "Come on! Show me your stuff! Don't make a liar out of my coffee cup." He shook a raised fist in challenge. Ranger Mark watched, thinking *That guy is as spacey and far out as me.*

Finally, the top ten feet or so of the berm gave way and rode downstream with the basalt train. The rest soon followed: sand, gravel, and boulders of ancient limestone showed up as whitish chunks within the downstream black basalt.

The march to the canyon rim was underway, and could only be stopped if the supply of new lava at JR ran out. Stone slipped into his version of acceptable prayer. *Damn it, nature. Don't let me down now. Complete this bucket-list wish, and I'll never ask for another favor. I promise.* Stone also talked to Superintendent Smith, who in turn publicly broadcast that no river-raft trips through the Grand Canyon would be allowed until he gave further notice. The U. S. Bureau of Reclamation, the federal agency in charge of the nation's dams, was notified that lava might soon start to create an obstruction in the Grand Canyon, effectively stopping the free flow of water between Glen Canyon and Hoover Dams.

Stone captured photographs and video of the advancing lava at least once a day, and shared the drama with Superintendent Smith, Chairlady Bond, and Bonnie. Tourist overflights of helicopters and fixed-wing aircraft maintained a steady engine drone during daylight hours. At ground level, groups of visitors were permitted to walk along the edge of the roofed-over lava river, guided by temporary National Park Service rangers who labored under the watchful(?) eye of on-site supervisor Mark. JR was perhaps the most thoroughly witnessed and photographed volcanic eruption, ever.

Just upstream of Vulcan's Throne, which sat perched like a cinder-cone sentinel at the very lip of the Grand Canyon, the lava seemed to hesitate, as though trying to decide whether to veer slightly right or left to get around this final obstruction. In the end, the Throne became girdled by a flow on each flank. These rejoined on the canyon side, allowing Bonnie to introduce her readers to the Hawaiian word, *kīpuka*. She used that newspaper piece to also explain the informal Hawaiian word, *semihoe*. Science teachers and their students at schools throughout the Southwest followed the JR eruption via on-the-ground visits and Internet classroom updates.

Early on the morning of Thanksgiving Day, lava began to spill down the walls of the canyon and into the Colorado River below. Stone watched in fascination as viscous molten basalt oozed down the precipitous slope, shedding solid chunks of quenched melt along the way. *Hot damn!* The solid stuff bounced and tumbled like a bag of marbles poured onto a rough hillside. Big chunks broke into smaller pieces and all sizes reached river level before their molten mother. Soon both were entering the river, and seemed to complain of their new wet environment by hissing and blowing off clouds of condensing steam. Boiling river water flashed to searing vapor bubbles that burst to the surface like a gigantic uncorked bottle of champagne. A mesmerized Stone watched for hours, and witnessed the formation of a new roiling-water rapid by late afternoon. He dubbed it the JR Legacy Rapid. It looked more river-runner challenging than its barely downstream neighbor, the Class 10 Lava Falls Rapid, widely considered the nastiest in the Grand Canyon.

Meanwhile, Bonnie was driving to Toroweap, with a turkey to cook with all the traditional trimmings. That evening, she and Stone celebrated their holiday feast in the trailer. "That was very tasty," Stone said, as he closed and locked the door. Harmonious tremor was their dessert that night.

17

A DAM IS BORN

JR Legacy Rapid had a life span of one month, a tiny bit of time in the overall history of the Earth. It was a rapid that no boatman would run. Nor would anyone have wanted to try if it had remained available. *If Lava Falls Rapid is a ten, JR Legacy is at least a two hundred. The water's rough, and its temperature would cook a river runner muy pronto,* Stone mused.

JR Rapid's reality, albeit brief, was recorded in perpetuity by a host of digital images, still and motion. With these and his recorded voice notes, Stone had the introduction to another research paper he could get into the peer-reviewed scientific literature. And of course Bonnie had the makings of an incredibly unusual and intriguing illustrated story to market with newspapers and magazines. She also now had competition. With the entry of a lava flow into the Grand Canyon, the ongoing saga of the JR eruption became news fodder for many writers nationwide.

The evolution from rapid to dam was the tale of a war between water and hot lava. In the beginning water was winning — continuous steam explosions quenched and shattered liquid and solid basalt as it entered the river. Water continued to flow between and around the accumulating solid rocky debris — in the manner of passing through a gigantic hot sieve.

Eventually, the top of the growing heap of shattered rock rose above water level. At that point the flow of molten basalt oozing down the canyon wall began to coat the emergent tumbled pile with a nearly impermeable solid frosting. Some water continued to leak through the cracked and tumbled base beneath that frosting, but the upstream current was reduced to a downstream trickle. On the upstream inclined slope of the heap, steam explosions continued when new lava met water. On the nearly dry downstream side, a solid thickening layer of basalt completely covered the busted-up rocky pile. Liquid lava, beneath a solid topcoat of insulation, began to flow down a virtually dry riverbed.

Stone cheered like a rabid sports fan, as he watched and recorded these changes from his safe perch near the canyon-rim campsite. Early on, it was obvious that the buildup of a lava dam was outpacing the rise of the accumulating reservoir of upstream water. Low river flow below Glen Canyon Dam as a result of the ongoing drought tilted that battle in favor of the volcano. Unlike construction of the Hoover and Glen Canyon Dams, no temporary diversion channels were needed as the basalt version of concrete was "poured."

There was no way that the national park staff could keep gawkers away from this unfolding and unusual event. When the NPS established barriers across the road into Toroweap, the public simply hiked to the canyon rim. Ditto for foot access at the South Rim of the canyon. Visitors there sat at the precipitous east lip of the tributary Prospect Canyon and enjoyed a real-time dramatization of a fictional version earlier created by a sketch artist for the *Belknap Grand Canyon River Guide*. On a typical day, thousands of tourists came to witness the spectacle. Superintendent Smith was proud of his park's visitation numbers, but worried about legal liabilities should accidents occur. Lawyers tracked the situation with glee, from the safety of their comfortably distant offices.

*   *   *

Once the dam appeared to be steadily and predictably growing and the lava flow on its dry downstream side was moving toward Lake Mead sans steam explosions, Stone decided to descend into the canyon for a closer look. *Piece of cake*, he figured. *I walked along bigger and faster-moving flows at Kilauea without gettin' hurt. This'll be one hell of a unique geology traverse I don't want to miss.*

"Hot dam!" he shouted to no one in particular from a canyon-rim perch. *Wasted pun*, he mused. The young risk-taking hotdog part of his character wanted to relive some of his Kilauea experiences. It had been four decades since then. Forty years of life without live lava. Way too long.

Bonnie was not enthusiastic about Stone's plan. But she realized that he would wallow in a sea of regret for the rest of their married lives if he didn't chase this to a climactic ending.

"Frank," she said as they hugged and parted company at the rim, "I want you back in my arms no more than a week from today. And I want you to be safe and unhurt. Okay?"

"I promise," said Stone, harboring a bit of uncertainty not projected by his voice, as they broke their embrace.

"Take care of my man, you two," Bonnie said to the recruited NAU grad students who were in the final stages of writing their volcanology theses. "He's the only one I've had for so long that I wouldn't know how to go about finding a replacement."

"Will do," came enthusiastic mixed alto and tenor replies.

Frank had selected these students thoughtfully. *If their thesis-writing experience is anything like mine was, way back when, they'll benefit from a few days away from the keyboard. Besides, they've been dealing with old dead stuff. I'll teach 'em a thing or two about live lava for comparison.*

The three were about to descend into the canyon, from a spot a bit west of Vulcan's Throne. They carried food, water, and other supplies for a trek planned to last no more than four days. One of the students, Hillary Sandoval, was a top-notch lacrosse player, in addition to being an all-around rock jock. The other, Mason Gardner, liked to pump iron and run marathons in his spare time. Both were in far better physical shape than Stone. He took advantage of their youth and vigor by letting them carry most of the load. In fact, they probably could also carry him if need be.

18

INTO THE HADEAN CHASM

Early January:

The new lava buried the Lava Falls trailhead at the lip of the canyon. It coated most of the steeply descending pathway, as well. Stone, Sandoval, and Gardner would have to advance slowly, finding a new route with safe footing as they inched down toward what had been river-water level. When they moved into the chasm, Stone felt an Alice-in-Wonderland moment tweak his consciousness — he was finally going to experience something as magical as his heady early career days at Kilauea. But his daydreaming was about to come with a price.

"Here we go guys," Stone said. "Into the heat. Follow me."

Sandoval and Gardner stayed far enough behind to carry on a conversation not heard by their professor. "This is so rad. Never thought I'd get to hike into the Grand Canyon to see an active lava flow. Yeah!"

Midway down, Stone crashed hard when a solid-looking foothold gave way. "*Mierda,*" he barked in deference to the students. "Guess I should watch my feet instead of the steamin' lava down below."

"You okay?" Sandoval shouted, scrambling with Gardner to help Stone to his feet.

Stone was quickly back vertical, his hands dusting dirt and grit off his clothes. "Yeah, sure," he said. "I'm fine."

His left knee hurt like hell from having flexed inward beyond the max angle that Doctor Crandall had set as a safe post-surgery limit. But he wasn't about to show weakness to the students.

"Let's keep movin'," Stone said.

As Stone brushed past Sandoval to once again take the lead, she said, "I didn't know you spoke Spanish."

Stone cracked a wry smile her way, and nodded his head in a yes motion. He got his backpack into a comfortable position again, and restarted the descent. They bottomed out with no more slips or falls.

The visible crest of the growing lava dam loomed a couple hundred feet above them, not far upstream from where they stood. Sandoval and Gardner looked ready and anxious to mount that hump. They could hear hissing and see rising clouds of vapor from lava meeting upstream water. Though a risktaker at heart, Stone knew it would be dangerous to climb that hot hill for a view of the rising water reservoir on the other side. "I'd love to see what's goin' on over the hill," he said. "But it's too risky. Let's just meander downstream and see what we can learn about the lava flow."

Stone's left knee was now making an audible click with each stride. He could feel something new with each step too, like maybe sinew was partly obstructed by bone — or some titanium steel hardware. Something in that knee joint must have been wrenched out of position during his fall. There wasn't much accompanying pain, but the click was something new and unwanted, and a reminder of his age.

Ten miles, three days, and innumerable knee-clicks later, they would camp at the foot of Whitmore Trail, a well-established path that would lead them northward to a Jeep-accessible road at the canyon rim. During those three days, Stone planned to teach a course in "how to safely interact with a slowly moving basalt lava flow."

They would crisscross the hot basalt repeatedly, from side to side of the now-covered river channel. When the lava advanced downstream, a roof of solid basalt had formed, creating a pipelike conduit for the underlying molten stuff. Just like the pipe feeding lava all the way from the JR vent. Only the leading tongue of lava was exposed as liquid. *Just what I saw lots of at Kilauea,* Stone mused. *Stuff there flowed miles and miles in tubes on its way to the Pacific shore. Damn we had fun stickin' metal rods through holes in a tube roof to scoop out fresh samples.*

The first time Stone crossed the roof of the Grand Canyon tube, Sandoval and Gardner hung back, unsure of how safe that was.

"Come on, you two," Stone coaxed. "Don't be wussies. Follow me. But keep movin'. This can melt your boot soles if you stand still too long."

Surface cracks in the lava-tube roof glowed red hot just a couple inches down, as evidence of that truth.

Stone stood on the south side of the channel, waving them over. Sandoval quickly crossed the hot walk. Gardner followed, once he saw that she made it safely to the other side.

"There," Stone said as the students joined him. "Not so bad, huh?! You'll have great stories to tell your friends back at NAU."

They were smiling the expression of excitement. They crossed back and forth a couple more times, and photographed each other while spanning a visible red-hot surface crack in the lava-tube roof. Stone watched, understanding their first-time enthusiasm for something that was old-hat to him.

"Here's a tale you can add from my early days of hot-lava walkin'." Stone began yet another story from his fond memories of life with Kilauea Volcano. "I got a little careless once at Kilauea. Laid my pack down on a tube roof so I could get at my canteen for a drink. Couldn't have been more than a minute before I retrieved the pack. All the plastic parts had melted."

Sandoval and Gardner were still in the *somewhat-shocked* stage of their introduction to hot-lava walking. They continued to share thoughts at a low volume that Stone couldn't hear. Then, after a few more crossings, they got boisterous, standing still on the hot surface until the odor of hot boot soles filled the air, enjoying their new sense of bravado.

"Don't get too cocky," Stone warned. "Come here." He motioned them to sit with him on a sandy stretch of the river's south bank.

"Here's another Kilauea story to digest," he began. "A geology buddy at HVO got a little too brave. Got too close to the edge of a stream of lava. Fell in up to his knees. He told me all about it when he got back from the burn medical unit on Oahu."

"You're kidding!" Sandoval said. Gardner shook his head in a "no way" motion.

"Nope," Stone said, in a matter-of-fact tone.

"He fell in and lived?" Gardner said.

"Yup," Stone answered. "He was lucky enough to fall backward, out of the hot stuff, right away. The short version of a longer story is he didn't suffer permanent leg damage. But the lesson for the rest of us is, don't step on a really really hot lava flow unless you're sure its roof is strong enough to hold your weight. So, you two, follow my instructions on this trip. There're no burn scars on my legs."

He pulled up the right, and then left pant leg in proof. *Got a newly screwed up knee joint, though.*

"Is that guy crippled now?" asked Sandoval, the super athlete.

"Naw," Stone reassured her. "He swims, plays tennis, golf and all that stuff. Could probably even play lacrosse if he wasn't as old as me."

Sandoval and Gardner weren't about to question the truthfulness of this senior professor to his face, although student scuttlebutt back on campus portrayed Dr. Stone as a sometimes jokester. Still, Sandoval and Gardner silently vowed to not tread on the new lava where Stone had not gone before them.

Halfway downstream to the Whitmore Trail, the three lava leapers caught up to the advancing front of the flow. The sight and rotten-egg sulfurous smell of liquid lava triggered more Kilauea memories for Stone. He unholstered his geology pick.

"Follow me," he invited the students. "And bring your hammers."

He led them to the snout of the slowing moving molten stuff.

Stone looked them in the eye and said, "You're now gonna learn how to collect a sample of liquid lava. Watch me."

With gloves and long shirtsleeves shielding skin from intense radiant heat, Stone walked to the oozing lava, swung his hammer hard enough to penetrate into the viscous melt and pulled to extract a baseball-size blob wrapped around the hammer head. He backed away, holding his tool at arm's length. The three of them watched the red blob solidify to a black mass within seconds. Stone giggled just like he had back at Kilauea during his first lava penetration.

"I'll shake this thing off the hammer and let it cool," he explained. "We can safely handle it a bit later."

He then turned to Sandoval.

"Okay your turn, Hill," Stone said. "And don't drop that stuff on your feet, once you've pulled it out."

She copied Stone's technique. Success. Ditto for Gardner. They sat on the dry riverbed's sandy south bank and waited until their samples could be handled.

"And those, my students," said Stone, trying to sound as professorial as he could, "are about the freshest and most untainted samples of basalt lava that you'll ever collect. Keep that in mind when you're studyin' old rocks that have weathered and stewed in various ways before you got to 'em."

Sandoval and Gardner carefully wrapped their fresh warm samples in dirty clothing and placed them carefully into their backpacks.

"Now the real fun starts," Stone said, eyes sparkling — wishing that Bonnie were here to share these relived Kilauea moments.

He stood and pushed a hand into the pocket of his blue jeans. "I brought some quarters for this lesson," he said. "I'll now teach you how to create a most unusual sample of fresh basalt. Watch closely."

He walked to the leading edge of the flow, the students a step behind him, dropped a coin onto the oozing melt, and pushed it part way in with the pick-point end of his hammer. He then collected a sample that contained the coin.

"We used to do this at Kilauea," Stone said. "Then we'd show the samples to tourists and explain how the volcano erupted money for her friends."

"Come on, Dr. Stone, "Sandoval said. "You're pulling our legs."

"Not at all," Stone said. "I'm serious. Ya know, Kilauea's in a national park, too. Eventually the rangers there made us HVO geologists stop 'cause some visitors believed us. Guess it was kinda tough for rangers to explain the science of a volcano that erupted money. I think too many of those Smokey the Bear types don't have much of a sense of humor."

Sandoval and Gardner were in full smile mode.

"But I'm guessin' you two do," Stone continued. "So, collect your two-bit samples and you can do a show and tell back at the department." He gave them quarters, and they did as suggested.

Their words of enthusiasm were mostly current student slang that Stone couldn't translate, other than know that they were hyped by his lessons.

"One more Kilauea story to share before we move on," Stone said.

It was lunch time. They sat on a sandy stretch where they could see the flow front advance and dined on dried fruit, nuts, and cured meat sticks — all washed down with what was now pretty-warm water. As they ate, Stone slipped into an Uncle Remus mode.

"Inside the national park at Kilauea," he began, "it's illegal for tourists to collect lava. Of course that rule didn't stop many from takin' a piece or two home. There's a whole literature about rocks later returned to the park superintendent with letters of regret. The typical tale was that bad luck visited the person after gettin' home from the volcano; that Pele doled out punishment for messin' with her home. The collectors asked that the rocks be scattered back onto Pele's abode, et cetera, et cetera."

"Sounds like crazy superstition to me," Gardner said.

"Yeah," Stone agreed. "But it still happens — a lot."

Stone gnashed another chunk off his meatstick and chewed.

"Collectin' outside the park is a different story," Stone continued. "It's legal. A favorite of local homeowners goes like this. First, get a round metal upward-flaring bucket — two gallon size or so."

Stone's mind flashed to his own metal bucket and its project list.

"Next, grab your garden spade and head to a slowly oozing lava flow. Use the spade to fill the bucket. Wait a few minutes for solidification and cooling. Wearing oven-safe gloves, invert the bucket to empty out the contents. Repeat this process until you have as many bucket-shaped pieces of basalt as desired."

His description sounded like a recipe from a cookbook. He stopped his story and gazed expectantly at Sandoval and Gardner.

"Well," Stone said. "What do you two think?"

"What's the point?" Sandoval asked.

Stone was ready for this sort of reaction. "First, my students of lava-collecting techniques, tell me the word that describes the shape of those newly created lava samples."

Silence. Head scratching.

"You two fail," Stone stated. "I wonder if you deserve to get grad degrees. Thesis defense time is comin' up soon. I'll be on the faculty committee."

Continued silence, with added worried looks.

"Frustum," Stone said finally, and then slowly spelled out that word. "Okay? Frustum."

"But not to worry," he added. "You're gettin' degrees in volcanic geology not solid geometry. You can count on me to vote yes."

Faces with wrinkled foreheads, morphed into ones with broad smiles.

"The point of collecting frustums of basalt was to decorate a landscape," Stone elaborated. "Some locals lined the driveway with 'em. Or used 'em as accents in a flower garden. All at no cost for a professional sculptor."

It was time to move on. Stone had stalled long enough for his sore knee to recover a bit. They donned their backpacks, headed downstream, and soon passed the front of the lava. From there on they walked along the axis of the dry riverbed. In addition to sand, gravel, and water-polished bedrock footing, they sidestepped the rotting carcasses of dead fish — not yet scrounged by the growing condor population of the region — and a still-sealed full ammo case "honey bucket" lost overboard by some river-running rafters. Stone was hoping to discover one or more sets of skeletal remains of the many folks who had mysteriously disappeared during their raft and boat trips down this storied river. No luck, today.

At dusk, they camped at the foot of the Whitmore Trail. They slept high above the dry riverbed. If the advancing lava arrived before sunrise, they wouldn't burn.

View to the northeast, eight miles downstream from Vulcan's Throne. Thin black lava flows veneer light-colored, much older, and deeply eroded sedimentary rocks of the Grand Canyon. Colorado River is exposed in the lower right corner of image. Part of the Whitmore foot trail is evident at the lower left.

19

BACK TO FLAGSTAFF

The heavily traveled Whitmore Trail was easy to follow and remarkably smooth. Sandoval and Gardner led the way up, jabbering incessantly about their experiences with live lava. Stone was happy to lag behind, where he could hide a noticeable limp, and his facial expressions of pain with each step. Click, click, click. Even his right knee hurt now, apparently from the extra effort needed to compensate for a weaker-than-usual left partner.

The NAU truck with a graduate student driver was waiting for the trio at the canyon rim. The students sat up front, Sandoval and Gardner regaling the driver with what they'd seen and had learned from Professor Stone. They shared some fresh samples of lava with him, but not those containing quarters. They would appear later, at some beer-soaked gathering of a bunch of fellow grad students.

Stone napped on his side in the backseat, curled in a posture of protection from something. They were back in Flagstaff by sunset. Bonnie greeted him with a hug and kiss on the front door stoop, as the students drove away.

"Hi lover," she said. "How was it down there with the lava and students?"

Stone freed himself from the hug and turned to go inside. "I'll tell ya later," he said. "Right now I want a double Cuba libre, a soak in the hot tub, and a long quiet night's sleep."

Which is what he got. Bonnie fell asleep a little concerned.

*　*　*

In the Stone household, the rest of January plus all of February and March were devoted to repair: trying to fix Stone's body and mind. The body part was pretty straightforward.

"Well, well, my famous volcano friend," said Doctor Crandall as she examined the new x-rays of Frank's knees. "Seems you've overdone it more than a bit. Your body isn't getting any younger, you know? You should slow down, if you want to live to be a truly ornery old codger."

Stone wasn't in the mood for vagueness. "Give it to me fast, and straight, Doc," he said.

"I take back the ornery part," said Crandall. "You're already there for that milestone."

For the first time in a while, Stone smiled.

"We can leave your left knee as is," she said, more serious now. "That click sound-and-feel isn't critical. We should take a new x-ray each year, but unless you badly twist that rebuilt knee, it'll outlast you."

"Okay," Stone said. "What about mister right?"

"In a word, shot," she said, her hand gently resting on that knee. "Soft tissue's gone. Take a look." The image was displayed on a wall-mounted screen. "It's obvious on the x-ray. Bone on bone, just like lefty was before surgery. I recommend total replacement as soon as you're up to it."

He was ready *now*. But it was another month of limping and Stone being a bit cranky, even with Bonnie, before Doctor Crandall had an opening for his surgery. She perched on her stool, did her usual competent job, and two months later Stone's physical therapy sessions had him back on his feet, moving with little pain. Just a somewhat slower pace while walking, and now with a scar welt across each patella. As promised pre-surgery, Crandall kept Stone's physical stance a bit left leaning.

When May rolled around and NAU broke for summer vacation, Stone stayed away from the university. He brooded at home about life in the slow lane — way too slow for his tastes. Any serious fieldwork was out of the question. Sure, he could hobble along on flat ground, but steep hills while carrying a backpack full of supplies could only be a memory. He was even reduced to not being able to practice the old aphorism he'd read somewhere as a teenager: "A true gentleman supports three fourths of his weight on elbows and knees while in the act of making love." He tried once, but the knee pain way outdid the sexual pleasure. Now Bonnie was up there. It was still good, but ...

*   *   *

When September arrived and Flagstaff once again celebrated its annual weeklong Science-in-the-City event, Stone was the speaker for the kickoff lecture. He entertained a packed house at NAU's Ardrey Memorial Auditorium with the saga of the JR eruption, and how it fit into a well-established pattern of eruptions at Toroweap and the series of about twenty lava dams they'd built in the Grand Canyon during the past several hundred thousand years.

In closing, he reemphasized, "It's happened many times before. And feel free to quote me as sayin' it'll happen again. Just don't ask for a specific date."

He paused, cleared his throat, and took a drink of water. Standard speaker techniques used to pump up self-confidence a bit, and let his listeners digest what he'd just said.

He pressed on. "If you take nothin' else away from this talk, I urge you to adopt the geologic, not a myth-based timekeeper as your clock of choice. Your offspring and theirs, generations into the future, will likely be treated to more JR types of events. Nature's in control. Not some amorphous mystic."

As a light-spirited antidote to blatantly advertising his view on the Christian Bible's clock, he now projected the Jiggles-versus-Rolf graph on a huge screen and quickly explained its significance.

"So, also remember," he said, "that Dobies may become increasingly valuable tools as the science of earthquakes and volcanoes moves forward." He then projected a photo of Mark and Rolf. That snagged the tension-easing listener laughter he sought.

The following week, Stone led a two-day field trip to Toroweap for a show-and-tell at the still-erupting JR vent. At the campsite view into the canyon, one could see the growing lava dam and a rising reservoir of water that was being slowly released from nearly dry Lake Powell.

During that fall semester, Stone worked with Stewart on two manuscripts for publication in the technical literature. One described Stewart's initial recognition of unusual earth tremor at Toroweap. The other dealt with ensuing collaborations that defined a link to Kilauea's signature of announcing a buildup to eruption and the present status of the JR eruption.

In addition to sharing their science, hours and days of close contact with Stewart drove Stone to better appreciate what a responsible person that family man was. Stewart worked diligently during his eight-hour days with Stone. But never more than eight. And never on weekends. That was family time and sacred to him. He doted on his wife, their now eight kids, and his church.

So what if Stewart chooses to believe in the myths of his religion, Stone eventually came to accept. *He's a devoted family man. Not a lazy ne'er-do-well. If only he hadn't exceeded the "replace yourself" child quota Bonnie and I believe in. That would have helped to contribute to humanity's chances for a long-term future on planet Earth. Well, time will tell, and I won't be here to see what the max human carrying capacity of our third rock from the sun might be.*

The second of their co-authored manuscripts for publication was in fact entirely Stone's writing. He described the onset of the JR eruption, the failed attempts to keep its lava from reaching Grand Canyon, and the continuing growth of the lava dam — a dam rising daily in height and breadth even as Stone wrote. *Someone else might have to write about the end of the eruption,* he realized.

Stewart could and would tend to his growing family, seemingly unconcerned about overpopulating Earth. Meanwhile Frank would monitor the eruption, its growing dam and reservoir, and offer advice on their possible future unwanted impacts on the USA's southwest corner of Earth.

In October, a special month in their household because of Bonnie's birthday, Stone received a letter postmarked Fredonia, Arizona. No return address. Inside was a handwritten note. He read it aloud, for Bonnie.

Hey, Frank. My pets and I are leaving Toroweap. Well, Finney died recently, so only three of us will be traveling. By the time you read this we'll be on the road. I gave Superintendent Smith my notice a couple weeks ago. With the JR eruption this place has become a zoo. An exciting and interesting zoo for many, for sure. But I prefer solitude and quiet. I've got a buddy who lives in a small cabin in the Big Sur area of California. I'll be moving in with him. It was great getting to know you, sharing a few pipes, and seeing how you do your science. May the rest of the JR eruption keep you smiling. Rolf sends thanks for making him famous. Be safe. Hugs to that special lady of yours. Peace. Mark.

During dinner at Horseman's Lodge to celebrate Bonnie's birthday, they raised glasses in a cocktail toast to Ranger Mark, Rolf, and Bertha. Later, at home, they secured some pipe fuel from spirited next-door neighbors and spent the evening recalling their pleasant times as newlyweds on the Big Island, in the shadow of Kilauea.

20

AS ONE RESERVOIR FILLS, ANOTHER . . .

Eight years later, the JR eruption stopped. There was no detectable advance warning. Nature simply ran out of magma. The "concrete pour" was complete. The lava dam stood fifteen-hundred-feet tall. Reservoir water was halfway to overflowing. Even at that partial-fill depth, all rapids were submerged for ninety miles upstream. Water would soon flood Phantom Ranch.

Eight more years passed. Phantom Ranch, and the nearby Bright Angel and Kaibab suspension bridges over the Colorado River were six hundred feet under water.

Farther upstream, a recently constructed multi-billion-dollar Escalade tourist attraction at the confluence of the Colorado and Little Colorado Rivers needn't worry about a fire hazard. The Confluence Snack Bar and BBQ Pit were under four hundred feet of water.

At Lees Ferry, the traditional starting point for raft trips through the Grand Canyon, the shoreline of what Stone called Lake JR met the confluence of the Paria and Colorado Rivers.

With just another foot of water, overflow would commence.

Downstream of the dam, the JR lava tongue had stopped on dry land at Pearce Ferry. Water level in Lake Mead was below the intake for generating electricity. It was also below the most recently installed intake pipe for supplying Las Vegas, Nevada, with water. The drought persisted.

*   *   *

The aging process on a typical human body was also persistent. Stone and Bonnie were now in their eighties, and they had succumbed to that reality by selling the house and moving into an assisted-living facility near Flagstaff's Museum of Northern Arizona. Their stand-alone cabin came with six hundred square feet of space for a kitchenette, living/dining room, and bed/bath suite. Mattress was of kapok-and-foam variety, rather than a water-filled bladder.

Stone of course brought his bucket to the new living quarters. He placed it on the concrete slab, just outside and to the right of the entrance door. It stood empty. If anyone happened to mistake it for a trashcan and drop something in, Stone immediately removed the unwelcome something. He insisted that the bucket remain empty. Its metaphorical list no longer existed.

A typical twenty-four-hour day in the new Stone residence was apportioned about equally among eating, reading, napping, watching TV, reminiscing, personal hygiene, and nighttime sleeping. In addition, until age ninety when his memory began to be visited by too frequent lapses for useful activities outside their home, Stone volunteered two days a week as a docent for the museum. The building was a ten-minute walk, just across Highway 180. He was a natural at a museum that featured geology, archaeology, and ethnology. And he was a natural with visitors because of his casual, folksy, yet fact-filled stories told, arms waving, in explanation of exhibits. The museum featured a live webcam view of the JR lava dam, and a weekly updated estimate of when the reservoir would overflow. Visitors were invited to guess the overflow date. The winner would receive a lifetime pass to the museum.

Without a steady source of new material for her Bouncing-with-Bonnie articles, Bonnie decided to write an in-depth book of the JR saga for a general readership. She had long aspired to become a novelist, rather than a writer who cranks out short report after short report. Not that her reportage hadn't been enjoyable and profitable. But it was plebian, relative to serious book-length non-fiction prose. This appeared to be her chance to step up a few risers in the world of authorship.

When she mentioned this idea to Frank, he encouraged her to go for it.

Piece of cake! Bonnie reasoned. *I've got access to all the inside science scoop and know the key characters very well.*

But by chapter four, when faced with further elaboration of an honest and accurate description of her life with Frank, which needed to be woven into the tale for heightened reader interest, she decided to abandon the project. She would have to research her diary for many of the details — details recorded over so many decades of married life. *It's been and remains a damned interesting fun-filled life. Full of unexpected twists and turns as we've navigated from recent college grads to middle-aged and now senior adults. But I'm taking all that with me to the end. It's mine, and Frank's, to treasure … not share with readers of too many ilks.*

Stone sensed that Bonnie was troubled as her sessions of typing became briefer, less frequent, and eventually stopped. For the first time in their lives, he played the role of sociologist and initiated a conversation that nixed the book project. Instead, Bonnie taught a no-fee once-a-week workshop for aspiring authors. She pooped out with that endeavor at age ninety, and joined her older spouse, now staying at home. There she coaxed him into daily sessions of reliving the joys of their lives together by daily readings from her dairy. Their motto became, *if you can't do it, read about it.* And they did. And they shared an additional life, vicariously, smiles galore!

Visitors who came to chat about the "old days" and describe current town activities typically found Stone and Bonnie seated on a loveseat, holding hands, smiling, and gazing at . . . Their most frequent visitor was Richard Stewart. He was now in his late sixties, and retired from his NAU professorship position. Stewart and Stone had bonded with time, through the shared JR eruption experiences, to the point that they actually now enjoyed mini debates about the strengths and weaknesses of science's "facts" arrived at through regimented and standardized methods, versus "truths" arrived at through faith rather than reason. Neither debater claimed victory along the way. But an enormous number of alcoholic beverages and herbal teas were consumed over the course of several years. Bonnie listened quietly in the background and smiled as the men of ideas clashed.

The early morning of Stone's ninety-fifth birthday arrived with one of Flagstaff's strongest spring blows, ever. May Day! May Day! For several hours, dust reduced atmospheric visibility and breathability to a hazard level for vehicles, aircraft, and asthmatics. By the time the wind ebbed, Stone's bucket was left atilt, overturned. As the sun rose above a hazy horizon, Bonnie stirred. She tried to awaken her man. He didn't move. Bonnie immediately knew that something was seriously wrong, from the lack of his trademark snore, which she had learned to sleep through during their first year of marriage. She phoned for medical assistance. Stone was pronounced dead in the ambulance.

One month later, she too died — mostly of loneliness, in addition to the wear and tear of time. As written into their wills, there was no formal ceremony in recognition of either death. The privacy they chose and cherished in life carried into permanent departure. Bonnie's diary was cremated along with their bodies.

The ashes were mixed together and spread near the JR vent, at the site of the jigglin' jug. Stone had arranged for Richard Stewart to carry out this task. There was one condition, however, that Stone insisted Stewart observe as he sprinkled ashes over the ground. Stone's last request was, "I want no words directed to a celestial being!"

Only Stewart knows if that request was honored.

21

EPILOGUE

Had Stone lived another five years, he could have watched the water of the JR Reservoir begin to overflow its lava dam.

On that day, The Museum of Northern Arizona sent notifications to two winners of life-time museum passes. The one sent to Claude and Fern Torlofsson, of Wendell, Minnesota, was "Returned to Sender." The Torlofssons had died. The other went to Leonardè Rockafortè of Flagstaff, a jazz pianist of considerable local and national fame. In return, Leonardè offered the museum a fund-raising concert, a fairly common gesture among residents of this bucolic, semi-isolated mountain town.

The initial water overflow trickled along the downstream side along the south abutment. Immediately, there was much discussion among responsible parties about whether to cease any release of water from Lake Powell in an attempt to stop, or at least slow the demise of JR Dam. There was concern about the potential for downstream damage if JR drained quickly. This concern was proved beside the point when calculations showed the rate of evaporation from JR Reservoir was less than the average annual rate of water input from the Little Colorado River. There was no stopping nature.

It took several decades of erosional downcutting and undercutting to allow free flow-through of water from Lake Powell to Lake Mead. Lake Mead Reservoir rose high enough to once again generate electricity and provide water to a thirsty Las Vegas population. Ironically, the ongoing drought that had arrived earlier with global climate change saved the destruction of Hoover Dam, and the series of smaller downstream dams, by creating a nearly empty Lake Mead bowl that could accommodate all that JR Reservoir had to offer.

Later generations of humans who visited exhibits at the Museum of Northern Arizona and Grand Canyon National Park marveled at the tale of Jiggles and Rolf. Eventually, as time dimmed human memory, what came to be thought of as ancient history seemed almost unbelievable. But there was that JR Volcano and a long, now-empty lava tube that led to a canyon wall, which was decorated with remnants of JR lava of the most recent Grand Canyon dam built by nature. And there were photographs and published reports that documented the exact timing of the JR eruption and its alterations to the landscape. One needn't accept the results of science's after-the-fact findings related to the study of pre-human volcanoes of Toroweap to "believe" in what had happened to the canyon as a result of JR's output.

Some centuries later, Flagstaff's daily news sources reported:

NAU SEISMOLOGISTS HAVE DETECTED HARMONIC TREMORS ORIGINATING NEAR GRAND FALLS.

Printed in the United States
By Bookmasters